MISSING IN BOCAS

Latitude Nine Degrees North

J A M E S   E .   M E R R I M A N

Missing in Bocas

CreateSpace
Charleston, SC
ISBN: 1519470533
ISBN 13: 9781519470539

Also by James E. Merriman

GateKeepers
Push Back
Bad Blood

This book is dedicated to Bob and Bobbie, whose infinite good humor and patience made the trip to Bocas del Toro an experience to remember.

CHAPTER 1

Sunlight reflected off the Caribbean, propelling blinding light and intense heat into every corner of the over-the-water bungalow. The aqua-tinted water lapped languidly against the support pilings. A rain-forest insect buzzed in an aimless pattern, and a fish flew across the water and landed with a soft splat. Bocas del Toro, Panama; nine degrees north of the equator; four in the afternoon.

"I feel like I'm in jail," blurted Stephanie Chambers as she threw down her book and lurched to her feet, knocking over the cheap plastic chair. She had spent the day trying to be polite, sensitive to Grant's feelings. He had tried hard to put together a memorable trip, but so far the memories were more like bad dreams. She walked over to Grant, who was putting away his snorkeling gear.

She wasn't mad, just tired, bored, and frustrated. She couldn't keep up the pretense that she was having a good time any longer.

"An over-the-water bungalow in Bocas del Toro sounded wonderful, especially after battling with Carlos Sanchez for so long. I was ready for the heat and humidity, but you didn't tell me the shoreline would be an impenetrable mangrove swamp populated by caimans, alligators, and twenty-two kinds of poisonous snakes. There is no beach—no place to walk. When you told me there was no way to town except by boat, it sounded okay, kind of cool, but you didn't tell me we could see all there was to see in Bocas Town in forty-five minutes and nothing would be worth a second look. After three days here, I have snorkeled off our deck so many times I'm on a first-name basis with the fish."

Startled, Grant looked up into her flashing green eyes flecked with sparkling gold, and then he looked away. He looked so sad, she almost felt sorry for him…almost. She was a doer not a sitter—an hour on the lounge reading, not ten days.

Grant stood slowly, like it was his turn before the firing squad. "Please, Steph, I'm just as disappointed as you are. The website didn't lie about a beach; it just failed to say there wasn't one. I'm as bummed as you are. I didn't realize all the islands in this archipelago were covered with mangrove trees that grow out into the water. The *New York Times* didn't say anything about that. At least we took the boat to a couple good places to snorkel; Red Frog Beach was okay, and you have to admit the food is good."

Having started to vent, Stephanie couldn't stop herself. "If you like dead coral and trash on the ocean floor, there are great places to snorkel. Red Frog Beach was full of backpackers in need of haircuts, a thorough cleansing with Comet, and a fire hose. We have seven days left in this place. Grant, this isn't a vacation, it's a sentence. I've already started making marks on the wall to count the days."

"Look, I tried," said Grant, pushing past her and getting a little testy. "I was hoping it would be like Bora Bora."

"You have about as much chance of getting laid here as a eunuch in a lesbian colony," snapped Stephanie. "Where did you put the Abuelo? I hate rum, but if I drink enough, maybe I can take a long nap and put another mark on the wall."

Grant didn't have anywhere to hide. There were only four bungalows connected by wooden walkways filled with so many loose boards and popped nails that, in the absence of total concentration, one risked falling in the water or impaling a foot. The single boat available to guests was gone. He was literally trapped. His only escape was to go snorkeling…again. He gathered his gear to the sound of ice tinkling into one of three glasses with which the bungalow was equipped. That wasn't the only shortcoming of their idyllic one-bedroom bungalow. They also had to supply their own drinking water and ice, and one couldn't live without ice because copious amounts of twelve-year-old Abuelo were a necessity of existence in this place.

A half hour later, Grant quietly pulled his chin above the bungalow dock to find Stephanie sitting at the table in only her bikini bottoms, her dark hair piled on top of her head. Her lithe five-foot-ten-inch body glowed under a sheen of perspiration. There was not an ounce of fat anywhere.

Stephanie was furiously writing, the bottle of Abuelo and an empty glass beside her tablet. She put down her pen, wiped a drop of sweat off her nose with a finger, and flicked it away, laughing to herself. She actually smiled for the first time that day.

"Hey, Grant, I see you. Come here; you have to listen to what I wrote."

Grant pulled himself out of the water, toweled off, and dropped into the chair next to her.

Stephanie, with reading glasses perched on the end of her nose, sat back and crossed her very long legs. "I think this is really good. At least it's how I feel about this place. Bocas del Toro: where human wrecks wash ashore to hide from themselves; where the jungle pushes those who live on the water's edge into dilapidated shacks perched precariously over the water; where a few picture-perfect beaches bake under a decade's worth of trash; where freighters on the horizon never come close to shore; and where ex-pats drown themselves in rum." She arched her eyebrows and looked at Grant.

Grant was grinning with his mouth clamped shut. He looked over her shoulder and then out toward the water. Then he began to shake. Finally, he could hold it in no longer—he started to laugh. After a while he was able to sputter some words.

"That was great...really great...Pulitzer stuff...Hand me the Abuelo...I don't need a glass."

He took a long pull, started to laugh, and spit out the rum. Undeterred, he took another swig.

Stephanie grinned as she watched him force the rum down. "Maybe I should be a writer...or not. Give me that bottle."

For the first time in two days, they both started laughing. Stephanie jumped up and grabbed Grant by the hand.

"Come on, last one in buys dinner."

They jumped into the clear, warm water, scattering a school of colorful fish.

Later, as they were drying off, Stephanie said, "Let's go into town for a nice dinner, maybe at Nine Degrees? Who knows, it might lead to something interesting."

"You mean my chances might be better than a eunuch in a lesbian colony?" Grant grinned.

Stephanie casually slid her hand down the front of Grant's bathing suit. "You don't feel like a eunuch, and I'm no lesbian. Who knows?"

CHAPTER 2

Grant watched the sun slip below the horizon from a small patch of shade and enjoyed a generous glass of Abuelo while he waited for Stephanie.

She was attractive, intelligent, and had immense strength of character. Sometimes, Grant knew her well; other times, he felt like he didn't know her at all. Sometimes—a lot of times actually—he thought he might be in love with her, but he wasn't sure what being in love felt like. At forty-five he had never been married because he had never found the right woman, or so he told himself. He had met many accomplished women, dated them, and bedded quite a few of them, but ultimately he told himself he was too busy or the woman needed too much of his time or it was too early for kids…or whatever. Whatever it took to end the relationship; he was usually the one to end it, but not always. Regardless of how the relationships ended, the only thing he knew about a broken heart was from love songs. One woman told him he was afraid to commit, another told him he was selfish, and one angry, teary-eyed woman even suggested he was a closet homosexual. Once, he thought he had the right woman, a Fox TV news personality—a blonde, naturally—but she had no interest in leaving New York for a ranch in Colorado. She was a star. When she had been fired a year later, Grant had mentally shrugged. He surely felt strongly about Stephanie, but love? At his age what was the point of marriage? Did he want to marry her? Would she marry him? At his age did he want kids? Did she want kids?

A slight breeze had kicked up and was cooling the inside of the bungalow when Stephanie swept out of the bedroom, bringing the scent of vanilla. She was absolutely stunning in a simple lime-green sundress that flattered her long, tanned legs and toned upper body. Her dark hair was pulled back into a ponytail, showing off big hoops of gold.

"My God, woman, you hose down really well," said Grant, quickly rising and leaning in for a kiss.

Stephanie offered her cheek. "I could do a lot better with some hot water and a clean towel. No one tells you that *ecoresort* is a euphemism for intermittent hot water and electricity, a lack of clean sheets and towels, and absolutely, under no circumstances, air conditioning."

Grant raised his hands defensively.

The sound of an outboard motor mercifully interrupted the one-sided conversation. The boat to town had arrived at the bungalow dock.

The eighteen-foot boat was called a panga. Years of exposure to the tropical sun had bleached virtually all the color from the boat and its tattered canvas top. There were two unpainted wooden bench seats for guests. Brown, the boatman, was indeed nut brown and stood in the rear of the panga amid empty motor oil and Coke cans with a big smile on his face. He was a Guaymi tribesman, whose family lived on Isla Popa, about a half hour away by boat.

Bocas Town was a pleasant ten-minute boat ride from their bungalow, but the ride didn't end at a dock in the town; instead, it ended at an isolated, dilapidated dock a little over a mile from the stores and restaurants. That was something else the website didn't mention. Their host tried to explain the use of this dock rather than the nice ones in town, but he made no sense. All Grant could figure was that he saved on gas and maybe a docking fee. Unfortunately, it cost them a taxi fare to get into Bocas Town.

As the panga approached the dock, Grant saw the whites of round eyes peering out of small, dark faces between the slats of over-the-water shacks that looked like they might fall into the water at any moment. Grant and Stephanie disembarked and carefully threaded their way down the dock, stepping over gaps in the planking. At the end of the dock, a short path

bordered by trash led them to the road, where they quickly found a sur-
prisingly clean taxi for the ride into town.

———

Nine Degrees was the classiest restaurant in Bocas Town. A polished
wood floor led to a canopy-covered dining deck, where candlelit tables
were covered with white tablecloths. Sailboats glided silently by, backlit by
the red-gold sunset. If their host wasn't so cheap, their panga could have
let them off right in front of their waterside table.

"Ah, Grant, what a pleasant breath of civilization," Stephanie said as
she inhaled the aroma of an Argentinian chardonnay.

Grant lifted his glass and said, "Here's to Carlos Sanchez—may he
never rest in hell."

"Amen," said Stephanie.

Stephanie studied Grant over the rim of her wine glass as he watched
a sailboat slip by and disappear soundlessly into purple, black, and gold
shadows. Physically fit in his midforties with longish brown hair and a
mustache, he looked like a cross between the Marlboro Man and a young
Omar Sharif. At six feet, he wasn't big compared to her five ten, but there
was an aura of competence about him. She knew men who were bigger,
better looking, and smarter...maybe. She had slept with a few over the
years, including the current president of Mexico; none had kept her interest like Grant Meredith. She was pretty sure he was in love with her. She
respected him, felt very strongly about him, enjoyed his company, and
certainly enjoyed the sex. When she thought about it late at night alone
in her bed, she thought she might be in love with him too. Whatever she
felt, it wasn't enough for her to let go of whatever it was in her head that
held her back.

"Grant, I've been thinking. We've done all there is to do here; why
don't we go back to Panama City. There are some resorts on the Pacific
coast that are not much more than an hour from the city, or, if you are

interested, I heard about a great tailor where you can get a custom-made suit and some shirts. What do you think?"

He took his time pouring some wine for them and then his face lit up with a smile. "I thought you'd never ask. Just kidding. Let's go back to Panama City and decide. Maybe stay at that new Trump hotel for a night and flush Bocas out of our pores."

They clinked their wine glasses together, and Grant excused himself to go to the restroom, which was down a long, dimly lit corridor toward the street.

CHAPTER 3

When Grant returned, Stephanie wasn't at the table. He looked around but didn't see her. He sat, thinking...she must have gone to the ladies' room. Where was she? He surveyed the room from his seat. A minute later he stood and looked around. Enough already. He crossed the restaurant, went down the hall, and knocked on the ladies' room door. No answer. He opened the door. No one was there.

Grant walked slowly back to their table, his eyes searching every table and corner of the room. She had to be here somewhere, but he couldn't see her. He stood by the table and grabbed a waiter's arm as he walked by.

"Have you seen the woman who was with me?"

The waiter looked at him blankly. "Lo siento mucho, no hablo inglés."

Grant had taken some Spanish in high school—enough to understand this guy didn't speak English.

"Es necesario un hombre habla inglés inmediatamente," said Grant.

The waiter scurried away, looking at Grant over his shoulder. He went to the bar and spoke to a man with long, stringy gray hair wearing a Hawaiian shirt. The man sighed, pulled his considerable bulk off the barstool, and made his way to Grant.

"What can I do for you?"

"I'm trying to find out what happened to the woman who was with me. I don't see her, and she isn't in the ladies' room."

The man looked over Grant's shoulder toward the water and the darkness. "She left."

"What do you mean she left?"

"A water taxi pulled up, a couple of guys came up to your table, and she left with them."

"She went with them? Was she forced? Did she struggle?"

"Yes, no, and no. It looked very normal to me."

"That makes no sense. What guys? What did they look like?"

"Sir, please calm down. You are disturbing my customers. Did you two have a fight? We see it all the time when too much sun blends with too much booze. Maybe she went back to your hotel."

Grant flexed his fingers—he wanted to grab this guy and shake him, but that wouldn't help things. He took a deep breath. "I'm asking you again. What did the men look like?"

Beads of sweat had popped out on the man's forehead, despite the light breeze. Refusing to make eye contact with Grant, he said, "I didn't see them real well."

"Come on, Mister...Who are you?"

"Gunderson. I own the place."

"Mr. Gunderson, did they look local or like tourists?"

Gunderson started looking around the room. The breeze shifted toward Grant, bringing a damp mist of expensive cologne mixed with sweat. Gunderson finally answered, still avoiding eye contact. "I couldn't tell. Everybody looks alike to me. Now you will have to excuse me; I have a restaurant to run."

Gunderson abruptly turned and lumbered away.

Grant stepped after him and reached for his arm but then changed his mind. The man knew something, but this wasn't the time or place to shake it out of him.

Grant spent the next ten minutes going from table to table, asking if anyone had noticed anything. Nobody had seen anything, or, if they had, they weren't talking.

Grant sat down at his table. Maybe she would be back shortly? But why would she leave without telling him? He checked his cell phone—no messages. Maybe she would call him? Shit, her cell phone didn't work in Bocas.

This couldn't be the work of the Sanchez family. Carlos was dead, and the rest of them had no interest in Stephanie or him.

Maybe...oh God. Grant closed his eyes tightly and tried to banish the thought. As a teenager, Stephanie had been in the car when her father, an army general, had been killed during a terrorist attack in Beirut. An Olympic prospect in the heptathlon, she had given up an athletic scholarship to UCLA and gone to school in France. When she graduated, she joined the CIA and was turned into a black-ops assassin for a number of years. What if someone from that life was looking to settle a score?

Maybe a kidnapping? But all she had to do was scream, cause a commotion, or, knowing Stephanie, fight like hell, and the kidnapping would have failed. This was no kidnapping. She would never have gone without a struggle. But, nevertheless, she was gone.

They had to have threatened her in some way, but why? What could anyone gain by taking her? No one knew them here...or did someone know who they were? It was possible that he could have been recognized; as the founder of BlackRock, the military contracting company, some opportunist might have thought he would pay to get Stephanie back.

He looked at his watch—it had been half an hour. Time was critical. What in the hell was he going to do? He was in a foreign country, he didn't speak the language, and he didn't know anybody. The obvious choice was the police, but if it was like in the States, they wouldn't act right away, but he had no alternative—he would try the police and take it from there.

CHAPTER 4

Two dim floodlights highlighted the police station's cracked stucco and peeling pink paint. *Police* glowed over the door in red neon. As Grant hurried toward the door, he stumbled and almost fell on the sidewalk, which had been buckled by the roots of a leafless palm tree. Regaining his balance, he rushed through the open door into an intensely humid atmosphere suffused with body odor and mold, which was stirred only slightly by a single ceiling fan. The room was partitioned by a battered waist-high wooden counter, behind which sat two policemen drinking beer and playing cards.

Neither of the policemen spoke English, and Grant's broken Spanish was inadequate to make them understand that Stephanie was missing. Finally, he was able to persuade the man in charge, who was as frustrated as Grant, to call someone in who spoke English.

Grant waited, alternately pacing the waiting area and sitting on a hard wooden bench between a drunken woman who babbled incoherently and a backpacker whose wallet and passport had been stolen or lost.

Grant had been an army ranger and helicopter pilot before getting a master's degree in Arabic studies from Georgetown University. Tatum and Hallis, a major New York investment bank, recruited him, and he had become its youngest partner in history before his reserve unit had been called up in the First Gulf War. He ended up working with the Defense Intelligence Agency before leaving to found BlackRock, USA, the most prominent military contracting company in the world. He was a player. Players weren't kept waiting.

The hands on the wall clock behind the desk barely moved. He couldn't believe it was taking so long. A woman had gone missing, an American woman…his woman. Where in the hell was someone who could speak English?

Finally, the police chief, Raoul Noriega, arrived. He was the only one on the force who spoke English. Noriega was not much more than five feet five with a narrow, pinched face and a sharp nose that made him look like a rodent. He stood behind the counter, drumming his fingers on the countertop with a bored expression while Grant hurriedly explained what had happened and asked for help. When Grant finished, the man actually yawned.

"Sir, please relax. I must ask…did you two have a disagreement, a fight?"

"Of course not," snapped Grant. "If we'd had a fight, I wouldn't be here."

"Sir, I have to ask because once or twice a week we get someone in here claiming this or that person is missing. Too much sun and liquor and there is a fight, and the woman stomps off for a while. They always come back when they sober up."

Noriega's condescending manner made his point. Grant was nothing more than a tourist; he was a foreigner who couldn't speak the language. He was tolerated because Panama needed his money. That was it.

"Officer Noriega—"

"Chief Noriega, if you please."

"Excuse me, Chief Noriega, she only had one glass of wine. She wasn't drunk, and we didn't fight—someone took her," Grant said, trying his best to control his frustration.

Noriega put his palms flat on the counter and straightened to his full height. He no longer looked bored or sleepy. His speech was tightly controlled. "Now, Mister…what did you say your name was?"

"Meredith, Grant Meredith."

"Mr. Meredith, these are the facts you have given me. You were in the men's room the entire time, so you saw nothing. According to Mr. Gunderson, a water taxi pulled up to the dock and two men got off, went to your table, and spoke to your woman. She left with them in the water taxi. Neither Mr. Gunderson nor anyone else in the restaurant can describe these men. No weapons were displayed. No one saw a struggle, which they surely would have. All your woman had to do was yell or create a commotion, but she didn't. Now, based upon these facts, you want me to believe she was kidnapped? It's at least equally plausible that she knew the men and left with them voluntarily. Don't you agree?"

Why couldn't the idiot realize what had happened? Grant put his palms on the counter and leaned across, causing Noriega to take a step backward. His voice was tightly controlled, anger boiling just below the surface. "Listen to me very, very carefully. She would never leave without telling me where she was going. At a bare minimum, she would have left me a note. For Christ's sake, I had only gone to the men's room. She could have waited another minute. The only thing that makes sense is that she was forced to leave."

"Maybe these men were old friends?" suggested Noriega, as if he hadn't heard Grant.

"What friends? I just told you we don't know anyone here." Grant's raised voice and tone left no doubt that he thought Noriega was the village idiot. By now the other policemen were watching the encounter, along with the other people in the station.

Noriega had taken all he was going to take. "Sir, I am not going to stand here and argue with you. I suggest you go back to your hotel and see if she is there. If she is not back by noon or so tomorrow, come back and maybe we can do something."

"But..."

Noriega slapped the countertop with his right hand. "Look, that's just the way it is. There is nothing I can do now. If you don't want to go to your hotel, why don't you look in the bars around town; you'll probably find her dancing the night away with friends you didn't know about."

Chief Noriega turned and walked away.

———

Grant walked up and down the two commercial streets, searching all the restaurants and bars for Stephanie until everything closed. Gray light had begun to lighten the eastern horizon as Grant stood alone in the empty street. He didn't think Stephanie had gone back to the bungalow, but he needed to rule it out. Grant found a water taxi that was just starting its day to take him out to their bungalow.

For the ten-minute ride, he held a glimmer of hope that Stephanie would be there. When he arrived, however, the bungalow was dark. He flipped a light switch, but nothing happened. He tried several others. The solar power must have failed, and their host was still asleep. There would be no power until the man woke up.

Fortunately, the stove ran on propane, allowing Grant to make coffee. He sat with his coffee as the sun pulled itself above the mangrove trees and began heating the day.

Stephanie wasn't going to suddenly appear at the bungalow, disheveled and hungover after an impromptu night on the town with people he didn't know. She'd made it clear she hated the place, but he couldn't imagine she would leave without telling him or at least leaving a note, and anyway, her clothes were still here. Even though she hadn't put up a struggle, someone had taken her. He was sure of it.

That pissant Noriega was right that he had no proof Stephanie had been kidnaped, and police usually didn't take missing-persons reports for forty-eight hours. The US embassy was in Panama City, and there wasn't much they could do without a missing-persons report. Still, he couldn't sit and do nothing. He would have to do basic police work and look for witnesses. Someone must have seen something.

•

CHAPTER 5

Grant took the 9:00 a.m. panga to town with the young honeymooning couple from the adjoining bungalow. Fortunately, they got on first and took the rear seat, leaving Grant in front of them. He was in no mood to watch them cuddling and cooing. His digital camera was clutched in his right hand, and from time to time he looked at the picture of Stephanie he had selected. Hopefully he could find a shop in this godforsaken place to print flyers with her picture stating she was missing and giving his contact information. He planned to canvas Bocas Town and then all of Isla Colon, if necessary. Someone had to have seen something.

An eager young backpacker told him about the Internet Café across from the police station. "Café" was a generous description. A single ceiling fan barely moved air saturated with body odor, sun block, and beer. To get to the counter in the rear, Grant had to navigate around three long wooden tables and bench seats filled with young people, who had casually dropped their backpacks in the aisles.

Delilah, the proprietor, was a middle-aged woman in black spandex shorts and a halter top that barely covered enormous, sweaty breasts drooping to her belly-button ring. She had an eagle with claws extended tattooed on her right deltoid, which fit perfectly with her hard eyes and an accent that was pure eastern Texas.

Delilah listened to Grant's request without any change in her expression and agreed to make fifty prints of Stephanie's picture and two hundred flyers to be completed within the hour. The price was exorbitant—cash only, no credit card. Grant didn't argue; he just paid. He had to get moving and keep moving. The more time that passed, the harder it would be to find her.

Grant found Noriega sitting at his desk in the police station with his feet up, a cigarette in one hand, and a Coca Cola in the other.

"Chief Noriega, I need help. I spent the rest of last night looking all over town for Stephanie, and then I went back to Bocas Villas, where we are staying. She wasn't there. Someone has taken her, kidnapped her. This is no lover's quarrel. It's time for the police to get involved."

Noriega slowly took a sip of his Coke and put it on his desk as if it were a fragile objet d'art. This was followed by a long, slow drag on his cigarette, which narrowed his face and made it even more rodent-like. He took his time pushing the butt through the hole in the top of the Coke can. Without taking his feet off the desk, he said, "I understand your concern, but there is nothing we can do now. There is no evidence of a crime. Please remember that, according to your witness, she went willingly. After forty-eight hours, we can put out a missing-persons bulletin. That's about it."

Grant closed his eyes briefly and said in a barely controlled voice, "Then come with me to Nine Degrees. I'm sure Gunderson knows something. He may open up to you."

Noriega slowly put his feet down and stood, leaning forward with his hands on the desk. "Mr. Gunderson is one of our most respected businessmen. He owns a hotel and several restaurants. It is not our function to harass the people who pay our salaries."

Grant couldn't believe what he was hearing. He took a step forward and pointed at Noriega. "Look, Chief, I'm telling you he knows something. I know this kind of guy; he'll open up if you just apply a little pressure. He doesn't want to get involved, but if you lean on him a little and ask him to do his civic duty and all that, he'll tell us something. Nine Degrees is just down the street; it'll take less time than smoking another cigarette to interview him. Come on, you're the law. You have to do something."

Noriega looked down at his desk. Then he looked at the ceiling. He took a long, slow, deep breath. His eyes were slits and his lips were compressed into a thin line. When he spoke his tone was low and tight. "Look,

Mr. Whatever-Your-Name-Is, you are a guest in my country and my town, and you will not speak to me in that tone of voice again, or I will have you on the next plane out of here. When there is an *official* missing person, and that can't happen for"—he looked at the clock on the wall—"another thirty-two hours, I will speak to Mr. Gunderson. Until then there is nothing I can do and, to be crystal clear, there is nothing I *will* do. Now, with all respect due a man with your manners, get the hell out of my office."

As Grant was walking out, Noriega shouted, "And stay away from Mr. Gunderson. If you harass him, you will end up in my jail."

———

Grant left the police station so frustrated he wanted to scream. This momentary frustration was gone by the time he crossed the street toward the Internet Café.

He'd just get the job done himself. That was the story of his life. Grant had learned at an early age not to rely on others to solve his problems. It had always been that way for him. His father spent nearly twenty years with the Eighty-Second Airborne Division of the army before being killed in a firefight along the Cambodian border during the Vietnam War. Grant was six years old when his mother told him his father would be coming home in a box. That wasn't how she put it, of course, but that was how he thought about it.

He'd had his first fight shortly after the funeral when another kid teased him, saying his dad killed babies. It had been brutal; he'd knocked the boy down and sat on his chest, crying in frustration, pummeling him until a teacher had pulled him off. It hadn't been long before his mother had married another soldier with three kids, leaving little time for Grant. As he'd seen it, he was always in the way.

For the next several years, he'd fought regularly and had several run-ins with the MPs but somehow managed to stay in school. His attitude and his life had changed when his uncle, a marine colonel, took him on a road trip to Gettysburg and other Civil War battle sites.

During the trip, his uncle had given Grant something he was sorely lacking—a sense of who he was and where he fit in the world. The Merediths were Scots Irish, not that they cared or paid any attention to that. If asked about their heritage, the answer was always the same: they were American—not this or that kind of American, just plain American. It didn't matter who your parents or grandparents were; all that mattered was who you were and what you accomplished. The Scots Irish culture was individualistic, stubborn, and rebellious. They didn't go for group identity. The southern Appalachian Mountains and the plains of America's western expansion built a fierce and uncomplaining self-reliance into an already hardened people.

During the trip his uncle had told him about the Scots Irish, from William Wallace, later portrayed by Mel Gibson in the movie *Braveheart*, to Andrew Jackson. He'd told Grant about the Scots Irish military tradition, which stretched back for two thousand years, and the fact that they served disproportionally in all of America's wars, including those like Vietnam, when many others did all they could to avoid service.

His uncle had summed it up by saying that the Scots Irish culture was family oriented, took morality seriously, joined and supported the military, and, his uncle had laughed, listened to country music. If that made them rednecks, so what; what counted and what set them apart was character and self-reliance. By the end of the trip, Grant had buried his self-pity and never again felt sorry for himself. He knew that he controlled his own destiny and could do anything he set his mind to and worked to achieve.

Grant never saw his uncle again; he died not long after their trip in a faraway place as one of America's finest, a marine.

———

Grant walked slowly across the street to the Internet Café to get the pictures and flyers. If he confronted Gunderson, there was a good chance Noriega would follow through with his threat. He couldn't look for Stephanie if he was in jail, so Gunderson would have to wait.

CHAPTER 6

Grant spent the rest of the morning and afternoon trudging up and down the dusty streets of Bocas Town posting his flyers, showing people Stephanie's picture and asking if they had seen her. She was surely a memorable woman, especially in this third-world town, but no one had seen her...or so they said. Several people who looked and acted like street-corner drug dealers barely looked at her picture and couldn't wait to have Grant move on. He had a sense they knew something, or maybe they just didn't want him interfering with their business.

He had been in every single store, restaurant, and bar—there weren't that many. He had also spoken to every water-taxi driver and boat owner he could find. What would he do if he could not find any leads, any information to pursue? Exhaustion didn't lead to clear thinking. His sweat-soaked shirt stuck to his fried skin, creating the sensation that if he took off his shirt, his skin would come with it. Despite the running shoes, his feet felt on fire and ached like he had been on a forced barefoot march. He had found nothing at all; Stephanie had vanished.

Grant wanted to strike out at Stephanie's captors—beat them senseless, torture them, kill them, something—but there was no one. She had vanished, and he had no way to help her. He could feel his frustration, ready to spin out of control, but that wouldn't help Stephanie; he needed to regroup.

Across the street was the Bocas Town Plaza, which was badly in need of some basic landscaping and gardening care, but at least its massive trees provided plenty of shade—a welcome respite from the relentless sun. Grant crossed the street and dropped onto a concrete bench covered with graffiti. He needed to plan his next move. The only thing that made sense was that Stephanie had been kidnapped. But if she had been, why hadn't anyone contacted him for ransom?

A short, skinny white man crossed the street toward him, carrying a brown paper bag. His shorts and T-shirt were faded but clean, and his sandals had been expensive but were worn out. His graying hair needed cutting, and he needed a shave. All of that was interesting, but what caught Grant's attention were his thin, hairless legs and pale skin. If the man lived here, he didn't appear to spend any time in the sun.

The man smiled at Grant and sat down next to him on the bench. He smelled faintly of alcohol. "You an American?" asked the man.

"Yes."

"Me too. You look beat; want a little Abuelo?" asked the man, extending the brown paper bag toward Grant.

"Thanks, but no thanks. Say, have you seen this woman around here?" said Grant, holding out a picture of Stephanie.

The man took the picture. "Wow. Unfortunately, no. And I would not likely forget seeing a woman like that in Bocas. Why do you ask?"

This guy was probably on his way to another drunken evening, but at least he would talk to him. No one else would, and Grant needed to vent to someone.

"That is Stephanie Chambers. We're visiting here, and she's disappeared."

Grant filled him in on what had happened and his singular lack of success in getting the police involved.

"I think the guy who owns Nine Degrees, Gunderson, knows something, but the police won't let me talk to him. The police chief, Noriega, says he will question him once the forty-eight-hour waiting period for a missing person is up. Christ, by then they could have taken her anywhere."

"That's true. Bocas is full of boats, Costa Rica is only an hour from here by boat, and Colombia is within easy reach."

Grant hadn't focused on that. Maybe he should find out where the water taxis go to drop off people in Costa Rica and ask around. Shit, if they took her there, they would never go to a public dock.

The man took a pull off his bottle of Abuelo and held out his hand to Grant. "Typical Bocas law enforcement. By the way, I'm John Scammon; once upon a time, I called New Orleans home. Been here almost three years now. Can't seem to get up the courage to go back to the States. Look, Mister…"

Grant shook the extended hand. "Meredith, Grant Meredith. Call me Grant. What do you mean by 'typical Bocas'?"

"Bocas has always been a backwater. The Spanish forgot about it. The region was generally ignored by civilization until the United Fruit Company took over the banana plantations around 1900. By 1934 a pest had wiped out bananas in the archipelago. There was no way to get here by road until the late 1990s. Now Bocas is supposed to be a great place for tourists. Bullshit. Maybe in twenty years, but for now it's still a backwater. Nobody in Panama City cares what happens here."

"How do you know all this?"

"I'm a writer, or at least I was when I came here. I had one novel published and had an advance to write another one set in Bocas. That was the idea. I did a lot of research before I came here, which is how I know this stuff. But anyone who spends time here and pays attention can figure it out. The cops aren't going to help you; they don't know how, and even if they did, they can't if certain people are involved."

"What do you mean, 'can't'?"

"This isn't the good ole US of A, Grant, it's Panama. We invaded the place in 1989, took Manuel Noriega to jail in the US, and installed a new government. Why? Bush the first said, along with human rights bullshit, that we sent troops to combat drug trafficking. Noriega had made Panama a center for money laundering and a transit point for drugs on their way to the US. How did the Panamanians take it? As you can imagine, not everyone was happy. The police chief here is Noriega's nephew. You can bet he is in someone's pocket."

"Whose pocket is he in?"

"Whoever pays him. I don't really know who. Anyway, it doesn't really matter. Unless you can find out who took her or why, well…sorry, it doesn't look good. But if it is a kidnapping, I guess they'll call you sooner or later."

Grant sat looking at his hands. He was trying to think, but his mind just wouldn't turn over. He hadn't slept well since arriving in Bocas and not at all for thirty-six hours. He was just about out of gas.

His reverie was interrupted by the arrival of another man, who greeted Scammon in a booming voice with an English accent. He was as big as Scammon was skinny. The buttons on his shirt were strained to the breaking point, and the shirt didn't even cover his enormous belly. A fringe of white hair circled his otherwise bald head. Mischievous light-blue eyes danced inside a bright-red face full of burst capillaries.

"Glad you brought a bottle, old chap. It's cocktail hour, and I haven't even had breakfast yet. Abuelo, I pray."

"Grant, this oaf is a useless ex-pat from London. Name of Peter Turnbull. His family banished him from England a decade ago, and he washed up here, where he is constantly up to no good," said Scammon.

"You're one to talk. Came here to write a novel. Thought he was the next Hemingway, yes he did. Got the bloody drinking down pat and hooked up with an African Carib woman up in Bocas del Drago who runs a restaurant and practices voodoo on the side. Hasn't written a word since," said Turnbull, taking Scammon's bottle and dropping to the ground in front of them.

"Well, at least I can go home," said Scammon.

"Jail—that's where your publisher will have you."

Grant held out Stephanie's picture to Turnbull. "Have you seen her?"

Turnbull's eyes turned guarded, and he glanced around and twisted to see behind them and across the street. "What's she to you," he asked.

Grant explained. "Have you seen her? Do you know where she is?"

Turnbull stood and looked around. "Let's get out of the open and finish this conversation along with this tasty rum."

CHAPTER 7

They led Grant to the Bocas Hotel, down its center corridor with polished wooden wainscoting, and out onto the canopy-covered deck of the restaurant, where they were the only customers. Not even a server was in sight. By the time they were seated, Grant's frustration had boiled over.

"Now tell me what you know about Stephanie—and I mean now," said Grant, jabbing his index finger at Turnbull.

Turnbull jerked backward involuntarily. He looked around again to be sure they were alone, and then he began in a whisper. "Last night I was having a quiet drink on the empty dock two doors down from Nine Degrees and I saw the woman in the picture in a water taxi with Pedro Martinelli and two other men."

"Who is this Pedro Martinelli?" interrupted Grant.

"He's the nephew of the president of Panama."

Grant sat back, stunned. Jesus H. Christ. They just get the Sanchez family off their backs and here comes another politically connected family.

"Who were the other two men?" demanded Grant.

"I don't know their names, but they work for Guzman."

"Guzman, El Chapo, the Sinaloa cartel boss", said Grant.

"Yes, I'm sorry to say the bleeding Mexican drug cartels have moved into Panama," Turnbull said.

Scammon intervened. "Grant, the Mexicans are everywhere in Central American now."

"Well, why don't you run them out, arrest them? Jesus, what is going on down here?"

Scammon patiently explained. "It's in all the newspapers that Ricardo Martinelli wants to amend the Panamanian Constitution so he can serve another term. Many think he wants to become another Hugo Chavez. When the new canal opens, the money flowing through the government will be astronomical. Money and power make the world go round."

"What does that have to do with Guzman?" asked Grant.

"Money. Martinelli needs a lot of money to change the constitution and get himself reelected. Panama has always been a transshipment point for drugs going from Colombia to the United States and Europe. It's a banking center with strict secrecy laws and anonymous corporations and foundations. It can end up Noriega all over again, but this time the United States won't have the guts to invade and overthrow the government.

"The leaders of Bolivia, Venezuela, Ecuador, and Peru are all ambivalent about cooperating with the US antidrug efforts or openly hostile to them. Bolivia and Peru are already making street-level cocaine. In fact, Peru is now a bigger producer of cocaine than Colombia. Think of all the container freight passing through the canal and going to the US and Europe; the opportunity to smuggle drugs is absolutely mind-boggling."

Grant interrupted. "Where are you, sitting here drinking every day, getting all of this information?"

"It's all public, on the Internet. I spend a couple hours every day in the Internet Café researching for the book I will begin to write when the rainy season hits. If I've saved enough money to buy a new computer," said Scammon.

"Okay, I get all this, but how does it tie in with them taking Stephanie?"

"I have no idea," said Scammon.

"Me neither," said Turnbull, taking a swing of Abuelo.

———

The Sinaloa cartel. Guzman. What in the world did they want with Stephanie? There had to be a reason. Grant knew that the Sanchez family controlled the drug trade in Mexico. The cartels all kicked money up the food chain to the police and military and most of all to the government. Stephanie and he had thought that with the death of Carlos Sanchez, their problems with the family were over. Maybe they had been mistaken. But why take just Stephanie? Why not both of them? Which was worse: a simple kidnapping or an abduction on orders from the Sanchez family?

He knew how many Mexican kidnappings worked. The kidnapper asked for money, you paid, and they asked for more money. When you finally stopped paying, the victim was killed, and the body was dumped in an unmarked grave. If necessary, he would pay to stall for time, but he had no realistic hope that merely paying ransom would get her back. He would have to find her and rescue her.

If the Sanchez family had her, she could already be in Mexico. Hector Sanchez was the president of Mexico, and the family controlled the country; finding her would be much more difficult than if kidnappers had her. Kidnappers would ask for money, and that would be an opening. The Sanchez family didn't need money. If they had taken her, it was for another reason. If it was for revenge, Stephanie was probably already dead, several hundred feet down in the Caribbean with an anchor around her ankles. If not revenge, what?

CHAPTER 8

Grant finished unpacking his suitcase in his room at the Bocas Hotel, which he intended to use as his base of operations. He didn't unpack Stephanie's suitcase. When he found her, they would be out of Bocas on a charter plane as quickly as possible. He would find her alive and take her home. He had to think that way. Giving up was not in him.

BlackRock, the military contracting company he had founded in the 1990s, had several accounts at the National Bank of Panama in Panama City. He had BlackRock transfer nine thousand dollars into an account for him at the local Bocas branch—not enough to raise any eyebrows, but enough to start paying for information.

His next stop was the police station, where he filled out a missing-persons report on Stephanie and waited for Noriega to come in from patrol. Given the involvement of Martinelli and the Sinaloa cartel in Stephanie's disappearance, he didn't believe the police could or would help him, but Noriega was the only safe way to access Gunderson.

Noriega arrived a half hour later and walked past Grant as if he didn't exist.

"Excuse me, Chief Noriega. I filled out the missing-persons report. Can we go and interview Mr. Gunderson now," asked Grant.

Noriega kept walking.

"Please."

At "please," Noriega turned around. "That's more like it. Okay, come on."

During the short walk to Nine Degrees, Grant asked, "Would you mind if I asked him a few questions after you are done? I have some experience in interrogations."

Noriega spun around and moved very close to Grant, enveloping him in a cloud of coffee, onions, and cigarettes, and thrust his index finger in front of Grant's nose. "Listen to me very, very carefully, and make no mistake about what I am about to say. I know who you are. You are the face of BlackRock, provider of mercenaries to the highest bidder. But know this: even God will not be able to help you if you cause any trouble in my town."

Grant carefully moved Noriega's finger out of his face and stepped back a pace. "You are mistaken. BlackRock is a military contracting company. We hire former military personnel and supply them to the US and foreign governments under contract with the US State Department and Department of Defense. We provide personal security to those who ask for it. We are not mercenaries."

Noriega snorted a stream of air from his nose, turned around, and headed for Nine Degrees. Over his shoulder he said, "Keep your mouth shut if you don't want to be arrested for interfering with a police investigation."

They found Gunderson at the bar having breakfast, even though it was early afternoon. He struggled to his feet and man-hugged Noriega. He avoided looking at Grant or acknowledging that he was even there.

"Raoul, good to see you this fine day. Something to eat or drink?"

"Not today, thank you. I'm here on official business, part of an investigation about a woman who may have gone missing from here two days ago," Noriega said.

"Sure, let's do this in my office upstairs."

Noriega turned to Grant and said curtly, "You wait here."

Grant sat down at a table and waited. This was a joke. These two locals were not going to help him.

A few minutes later, Noriega returned alone and confirmed his suspicions.

"Just like he told you. She appeared to leave voluntarily, and he cannot describe the men she left with. I'll post a bulletin and let you know if anything turns up."

Grant's eyes narrowed to slits, and his mouth became a hard, thin line. He clenched his fists so hard that his fingernails bit into the palms of his hands. Noriega's eyes widened, and he took a step back involuntarily, raising his hands to protect himself. Grant took a deep breath and willed himself not to hit Noriega. It wouldn't change anything, and he would end up in jail. He wheeled around without another word and left Noriega standing there. Noriega collapsed into a chair, pulled a handkerchief from his pocket, and wiped the sweat off his face.

CHAPTER 9

During the hundred-yard walk to his hotel, Grant forced himself to take deep breaths and exhale slowly. He was frustrated, angry, and fearful for Stephanie. None of that was going to do him or Stephanie any good. There was a time and place for all those emotions, but this was not it. He hated the word *proactive*, but that was what he needed to be. He needed help, and it wasn't going to come from the local police. What he needed more than anything was to calm down and think.

Grant walked down the hotel's narrow hallway from the street to the dock, where he got a Balboa from the bar and went to his room. There he settled in at the small desk with his phone, a pad of paper, and a pen. His first call was to the US embassy in Panama City. Perhaps the embassy could put some pressure on the government to help.

An hour later Grant stood on the small balcony of his hotel room, staring out at the water. The US embassy couldn't help. He had just filed a missing-persons report, and he was supposed to allow the police a reasonable amount of time to do their job.

A former president of the United States, a BlackRock board member, had put in a call to the State Department, which suggested contacting a nonprofit organization called Missing Abroad. No help there.

Finally, he had spoken with Peter Chastain, CEO of BlackRock. All he'd had to offer was manpower to help canvas the area, but that would no doubt cause political and perception problems in such a small town. Grant had reluctantly agreed that the risks to the company outweighed any good they could do. However, if he found Stephanie and needed help to rescue her, the company would spare nothing to help rescue one of its own—Panamanian sovereignty and bad publicity be damned.

Grant dumped his untouched beer in the bathroom sink and dropped the bottle in the wastebasket. It was twilight, a good time for a walk and to think. The main street was crowded with people in a holiday mood. It was Carnival, and people in costume were drinking from beer bottles, dancing, parading up and down the street, and generally carrying on to loud music from speakers set up on a flatbed truck. It wasn't Rio or New Orleans, but the people were certainly enjoying themselves.

As Grant crossed the street, he saw two young men in a shadowed doorway. One, who looked like a foreign backpacker, exchanged money for a bag of what was probably marijuana with a Bob Marley wannabe sporting dreadlocks to his waist and a faded T-shirt with a peace symbol. A drug deal. Nothing unusual in Bocas Town or anywhere else for that matter, but it gave Grant an idea. He doubted this street dealer knew anything about Stephanie's whereabouts, but if he could work his way up the distribution chain, he might find someone who did.

Over the next half hour, Grant used his cell phone to photograph the dealer sell baggies of marijuana to three different people. When the dealer left his doorway, Grant followed him to a dilapidated shack on an empty back street. Taking a chance that no one else would be inside, Grant followed him through the door.

The startled drug dealer wheeled around. "What the fuck you doin', man?"

"We need to talk," said Grant calmly.

"No we don't, asshole. Git outta my crib."

Grant bitch-slapped the drug dealer. The man staggered backward and grabbed the back of a chair to keep his balance. He rubbed his cheek and glared at Grant.

"Christ, what the fuck do you want?"

"Information."

"I got nothing to say."

Grant held up his cell phone with his left hand and showed him a picture of one of his drug sales. "The police will be interested in your little pissant drug business."

The man smiled. "Fuck you. You got nothin'. They get their cut. Fuck off."

"Very well," said Grant, grabbing the dealer's throat in a grip that caused the man's eyes to bulge. "Sit."

The dreadlocked dealer slid down in the chair, and Grant expertly tied him to it with electrical cord pulled off two of the lamps in the room.

"What's your name?" asked Grant.

"Fuck off."

Grant backhanded him across the nose, releasing a stream of blood.

"What's your name?"

"John," said the man, blinking back tears.

Grant didn't believe him, but that didn't matter. He held a picture of Stephanie in front of the man. "Now, John, have you seen this woman?"

"No," stuttered John.

Grant reached out and squeezed John's nose, eliciting a scream followed by uncontrollable sobbing. John was having trouble catching his breath.

"I'm sure you've seen this in the movies. You can tell me what I want to know now or a few minutes from now after I break a few of your fingers and maybe a leg or two. Do you believe I would do that to you?"

John couldn't speak; instead, he bobbed his head up and down.

"Last chance. Have you seen her?"

"No…honest, mister, I haven't seen her, I promise."

Grant casually sat on the edge of a table and studied John. His veneer of toughness had crumbled quickly. He wasn't strong or brave. He was probably telling the truth.

"Who do you work for?" asked Grant. He could see the whites of the man's eyes as the question registered.

"Honest, I don't know. Please don't hit me," blubbered John.

Grant sighed deeply, stood, and walked behind John, where he grabbed his left index finger and bent it back just short of the breaking point.

"Tell me."

John's eyes filled with tears, and the words rushed out. "Please, mister, I don't know. I meet someone who comes here in a boat every Monday bringing product. Not the same guy all the time. They don't give names, and I sure don't know how to contact them. I took over for a guy who went back to Panama City. He told me when and where to meet the boat. Honest…I don't know nothin'."

Grant released his finger. He believed him. Compartmentalization was the key to success in the drug business. It had been a long shot anyway.

"I'm going to loosen the wire. You ought to be able to work yourself free in a few minutes. It's six thirty. Don't come out for a half hour. If you tell anyone about this, I or one of my associates will cut your throat. Got it?"

John bobbed his head enthusiastically.

Grant kicked himself. If the guy went to the police, Grant was going to be in serious trouble. The least Noriega would do is run him out of town. The odds of a street dealer knowing anything helpful were virtually nil. His need to do something was outweighing common sense, and trying to interrogate Gunderson was out of the question.

CHAPTER 10

Grant's next stop was Toro Loco, a waterfront bar just down the street from Nine Degrees and across from the plaza. Here he found Scammon and Turnbull with a half-empty pitcher of sangria on the table. After Grant ordered a club soda, he noticed that Turnbull was looking at him with a sly grin on his face and a mischievous sparkle in his light-blue eyes.

"Okay, Turnbull, out with it," said Grant.

"Well, I'm honored to be in the presence of such a distinguished personage."

"What in the hell are you talking about?" asked Grant.

Turnbull looked at Scammon and winked. "Mr. Grant Meredith, former Wall Street investment banker, army ranger, First Gulf War veteran, and founder of BlackRock, the preeminent military contracting firm in the world. Friend of an ex-president of the United States and member of the ruling class. Quite a resume, I might add."

Grant looked at Scammon, who was nodding in agreement. "Who told you all this?"

"I'm good friends with Delilah, who owns the Internet Café—"

"Intimate, bosom buddies, I would say, no pun intended," interjected Scammon.

Turnbull held up his hand. "Jealously will get you nowhere. I happen to like women with some meat on their bones, not like that skinny voodoo queen of yours."

An involuntary picture of Turnbull and Delilah in bed flashed before Grant's eyes. Frightening. He pushed it away as quickly as it had come.

"Cut it out," snapped Grant. "What did she say?"

"Well, your friend Chief Noriega used one of her computers to surf the Internet, and after he left she checked out the sites he had visited—after all, it's a public place, no guarantee of privacy posted anywhere. He had been researching you. She was interested, so she read about you and told me. It's not often we get important people such as yourself in Bocas."

Grant wasn't sure what to make of this. Noriega probably had access to the Internet in the police station. It was curious that he would use a public computer to research him. Given the likely small-town gossip, it wouldn't be long before everyone knew who he was. It might help or it might hurt. He would find out.

"Look, guys, focus please. I want to find Martinelli or one of the other men who took Stephanie. Preferably Martinelli—he's probably running the show. Where would he be staying?"

Both men filled their glasses and took healthy swallows of sangria. Some of Turnbull's dribbled out of the corner of his mouth and onto his shirt, where it nestled in the company of other stains.

"Not in Bocas Town, for sure," said Scammon. "Too small and nothing grand enough for a guy like that."

"How about out at Bocas del Drago?" offered Turnbull.

"Not there. Astrid, my woman, would know it and would have told me," said Scammon. "But maybe one of those estates on the eastern side of the island between here and there?"

"How about Bastimentos?" suggested Turnbull, stifling a burp. "There are some quiet, pretty decent villas in the Red Frog Beach development and on Juan Brown Point."

"That's a lot of ground to cover," said Grant. "How about asking a local realtor?"

Both Scammon and Turnbull laughed.

Scammon spoke first. "Not in Bocas Town. Everything is for sale by owner. Fancy places would have a Panama City broker."

"What about Guzman's people? Where would they be staying?"

"No idea," responded Turnbull, "but they would probably go to Barco Hundido from time to time. Big nightlife spot."

CHAPTER 11

Needing to clear his head, Grant went for a grueling five-mile run, dodging taxis that seemed determined to run over anything on or near the road. Afterward, a cold shower and a two-hour nap got him ready for Saturday night in Bocas Town.

At ten that evening, he crossed the plaza and entered Barco Hundido, a thatched-roof, open-air bar throbbing with the intoxicating reggae beat of Burning Spear a.k.a. Winston Rodney. Dense, humid air was thick with the smell of marijuana, sweat, and beer. Multicolored strobe lights alternately illuminated and plunged a packed crowd of sunburned backpackers from around the world into darkness. The dance floor was filled with intoxicated patrons laughing, shouting, and swaying to the music.

Grant threaded his way through the revelers to a stool at a back corner of an elevated bar with an excellent view of the interior as well as the street entrance. He ordered a beer and surveyed the crowd. The flashing lights made it difficult to see clearly, but after a few minutes, he was sure the Mexicans weren't there.

Half an hour later, a party of four people came in from the street. The group included two dark, hard-looking men in slacks with full-cut shirts hanging over their belts, no doubt to cover guns at the smalls of their backs. Grant hadn't seen any hard-looking men since he arrived in Bocas, and these men certainly weren't tourists. They had to be the El Chapo's men. The women, one in a short, low-cut sundress and the other in white shorts, were in high heels. This was not a group of backpackers seeing the world.

The taller man spoke briefly with the bouncer, a huge black man, and pointed at a table in the corner occupied by a group of tank-topped long-haired surfers. The bouncer went to the table and appeared to be asking the surfers to move. When one of the young men protested, the bouncer took his arm in a ham-sized hand, lifted him off the stool, and walked him across the room. His companions meekly trailed behind.

The four newcomers took their table, and pitchers of margaritas arrived. After a while, the women danced with each other in such a suggestive manner that it caused revelers to step back and give them room.

Grant pulled a waiter over and asked who the dancers were. The waiter said the women were probably Colombian prostitutes, but he got nervous and hurried away when Grant asked about the men.

Grant nursed another beer as he watched the group from the corner of his eye. Later, one of the women danced with a braless blonde girl in a cropped white tank top with "PINK" stenciled across her chest. The blonde was part of a group of young people Grant had seen in a surf shop earlier in the day.

Around midnight Grant saw the waiter he had questioned speaking into the ear of the taller of the Mexican men. Both men then looked directly at Grant. The waiter left, and the Mexican continued to stare at Grant. After a moment, he spoke briefly with the other man, and both focused hard eyes on Grant.

Taking the hint, Grant left a twenty on the bar and, doing his best imitation of a drunk, struggled up slowly off his stool, stumbled, and almost fell. He staggered toward the street exit, using the railing to balance himself. Outside, the strobe lights provided some light under an overcast sky hinting at rain. Grant continued to stumble across the street and into the plaza, where he disappeared into blackness under the massive trees. He stood next to a tree trunk and waited for the Mexicans to come out of the bar.

About one in the morning, they came out and walked down the middle of the street toward the town dock. Grant followed on the sidewalk about thirty yards behind them, hugging the shadows. The two women walked unsteadily in their high heels, carrying on an animated conversation in Spanish punctuated with hand and arm gestures. In stark contrast, the two men walked steadily, ignoring the women, surveying the street ahead, and turning occasionally to check their rear. They weren't drunk, and they weren't out for a midnight stroll—they were trained, aware of their surroundings, dangerous. They reached a dock at the west end of town, where a twenty-foot panga driven by another man waited for them. They piled in and sped away, going where, Grant had no idea.

Grant turned and bumped into the bouncer from Barco Hundido. The black man was six feet tall and at least two hundred and fifty pounds. His face glistened with sweat in the moonlight. Grant backed away and started to excuse himself when the man reached out with massive hands and thick fingers, grabbing Grant by the shirtfront, jerking him in close, and lifting so that the shirt dug into Grant's armpits.

"Little mon, why yuh followin' muh frens?"

Instinct and years of training took over. Without conscious thought, Grant brought his arms up between the black man's massive arms and, using all the strength in his arms and shoulders, exploded his arms outward, breaking the big man's grip. Instantly, Grant drove the knuckles of his right hand into the man's larynx, feeling it collapse. As the big man's hands went to his throat, Grant stepped back and kicked him in the crotch. He collapsed, and Grant disappeared into the darkness.

Back in his hotel room, Grant splashed his face, neck, and arms with cold water and pulled a beer from the minibar. He moved to the balcony and stood staring at the moonlit Caribbean as he sipped the beer, savoring its coldness.

How could he have been such an amateur? He had underestimated the Mexicans, and that was unforgivably stupid. He was lucky to be alive. The big man would need a hospital, and that meant Panama City. At least he would be out of the way for a while, but he may be able to alert the Mexicans. Of course, the Mexicans would have to expect him to be looking for Stephanie, so maybe nothing had changed. He would have to assume they would be more careful, and it was unlikely he would find them in public again. He would have to find another string to pull. He replayed the evening over and over in his head and finally found a string. Exhausted, he propped a chair under the doorknob and dropped onto the bed fully clothed.

CHAPTER 12

Early the next morning, Grant ate breakfast next to a dive shop directly across from the surf shop on Calle Third. A group of people who were waiting for the morning boat to go surfing were milling in and around the shop. Promptly at nine, the surfers grabbed their boards, crossed the street, and piled into their boat for the morning excursion to Paunch, a popular surfing beach.

Grant got a coffee to go, crossed the sand-coated asphalt road to the surf shop, and entered a humid atmosphere of suntan lotion and body odor. Behind the shop's plate-glass window was a big open room with several worn-out sofas in the middle of the floor. One wall held surfboards for rent, and the others were covered with surfing posters. A flat-screen TV behind a counter was running surfing movies with Beach Boys music in the background.

The blonde girl from the night before was alone in the shop, cleaning up empty cups and other debris left by the surfers. Long legs and small breasts were accentuated by low-rise shorts and a crop top. When she bent over to pick up a cup, Grant saw a surfer-girl tattoo on her lower back that disappeared into her shorts.

"Like, good morning, dude, if you're here to surf this morning, you're way late. They left. We got another totally cool trip launching at two this afternoon."

"Great," said Grant. "What part of the valley are you from?"

"Like, Calabasas, ya know, where they make all the porn. That stuff is totally gross. I mean, who wants to watch all that humpin' and bumpin'? How didya know I was from California?"

"You look like a surfer girl, sound like a surfer girl, and that surfer-girl tattoo on your lower back is pure California. Plus, you're here alone and there's Beach Boys music on the sound system."

"Awesome! You should be a detective, dude."

Grant settled on the arm of a shabby sofa, and they talked about surfing and the shop while she cleaned up. Grant was careful to let her do most of the talking, and she did like to talk. After she finished her cleanup, Grant got her some coffee from across the street, and they sat on sofas across from each other with their feet on a scarred wooden coffee table. From time to time, a customer wandered in to inquire about renting a board or taking a surf trip. Grant just relaxed and glanced at the surf magazines strewn across the table. She kept coming back to her sofa. Grant sensed that she was lonely and wondered what she was doing in Bocas. Valley speak aside, she seemed like a young woman drifting through life.

"What brought you to Bocas?" asked Grant.

"Duh, the surf, dude—it's rad. Tried Hawaii, Nuquí in Colombia, and Hermosa in Costa Rica, but, like, it was way expensive, and the tourists, I mean, dude, it was gross, you know what I mean?"

"Sure. What about Malibu?"

"Too close to my old man. I mean, he was so uncool…as if he had some right to rule my world. You know, buggin' me about gettin' a job and other bogus stuff. He just got totally wacked out and started makin' a major deal about where I was goin' and who I was with. I mean, no way was it righteous. It was so lame, I had to ditch So Cal, you know."

Grant spent some more time commiserating with her about overbearing parents and their unrealistic expectations. He had been talking with her on and off for about two hours, and it was getting close to the time when the morning trip would be returning and the afternoon surfers arriving. It was time.

"I saw you at Barco Hundido last night. Cool place. Do you hang there often?"

"Only on weekends. It's pretty lame during the week sometimes."

"You were dancing with a really hot gal in white short shorts. She didn't look like a local or a tourist." He waited, but only for a second before she filled the vacuum.

"Oh yeah, that was Alisha, she's rad. Met her in Nuquí when I was there. She was with a real barf that drank all day and passed out about dark. We had some cool times and got real close. I mean, well, you know, most of the guys I hook up with are just in it for themselves. I mean, gag me with a spoon if I'm not right, but they just don't get it. Slam bam and all that sketchy stuff. Now Alisha, she is some kind of sweet, I mean, in bed, she can put any guy to shame. No offense. I mean, you know, I didn't mean, well, don't take it personal, as if, I mean, I didn't mean you—"

"No offense taken. What's she doing here?"

She rushed on. "Oh, she works for some gnarly narco in Medellin. He sets her up with guys. She likes it—nice clothes, travel, and money—but she thinks Bocas is barf city, not enough action for her...whateva. But she's only got another day or two here."

"Where is she staying?"

"Some fancy digs up in the jungle at Red Frog Beach over on Bastimentos. She, like, totally hates it."

Grant continued chatting with her until the morning surfers got back. Then he slipped out and went looking for Scammon.

CHAPTER 13

Grant hustled to the plaza looking for Scammon, but he wasn't there. He knew Turnbull spent a lot of time on the shaded dock that was the waterfront side of a building in the throes of an abandoned rehabilitation project just down from Nine Degrees. It was on the water, it was quiet, and no one bugged him. It was a good place for a solitary drinker. Grant found him there, sitting in a folding chair that sagged under his weight, sipping a bottle of Coca Cola.

"Hey, Turnbull, I can't believe you're drinking a Coke."

"Don't believe your eyes, matey," he said as he lifted a bottle of Abuelo that his ample bulk had obscured.

The whites of Turnbull's eyes were solid red. He had missed two patches of whiskers the last time he'd shaved, and there were two buttons missing from his shirt where his belly protruded.

Grant knelt in front of him. "I need your help."

Turnbull nodded.

"Where can I find a gun?"

"Guns are legal, but tourists can't buy one."

"Buy one for me."

"Got to get a permit first. Takes a couple of days. Anyway, there are no gun shops in Bocas."

"There's always somebody who will sell a gun. Who do I ask? I'll pay whatever they want."

Turnbull burped, poured some Abuelo into his Coke bottle, put his thumb on the mouth, turned it upside down, righted the bottle, and took a sip. "Ask Delilah."

Turnbull set his bottle of rum and Coke down, burped, and closed his eyes. "Time for a little nap."

———

Grant found Delilah behind the counter in the Internet Café. She still had on black spandex shorts, but this time they were topped with a very tight black tank top. Her braless breasts—knockers, Turnbull had called them—rested on a roll of belly fat. Grant asked if he could speak with her privately.

She led him through a curtain of beads into a back room where a ceiling fan turned lazily, doing little but stirring dust motes in the air. A dusty pressed-wood desk was piled high with papers of some sort. In the corner there was a single unmade bed with dirty sheets.

Delilah placed her prodigious rump on a corner of the desk and looked at Grant with her hard eyes. "What ken I do fer yuh?"

"I understand you may be able to help me buy a gun."

Delilah pulled her arms up, cradling her breasts. The nipples seemed to be staring at Grant through the thin fabric. She looked at him for several moments, turning her head from side to side, slowly observing him. "Why yuh needin' a gun?"

Grant considered what, if anything, to say. This woman had obviously been around the track several times and had a well-developed bullshit meter.

"You printed the flyers; I'm looking for Stephanie. I think she has been kidnapped by some very bad men. When I find them, I'm going to do whatever it takes to free her."

Delilah hocked up some phlegm and spit it into the trash can by the desk. "It's gonna take a lot…if'n yuh find her."

"What do you mean?"

"Turnbull tole me the cartel gotten her. The possibilities ain't that great. One, they have uses for good-lookin' women, who come back, if at all, crazy or wishin' they was dead. Two, they ask for ransom, which I hear they ain't done. Which leaves us wit three, she's dead. Oh yeah, there's four, they hear yur lookin' fur 'em or yuh find 'em and yuh get dead. Sorry, them's the facts, pure and simple."

Grant's lips compressed into a thin line and his eyes narrowed. "Can you get me a gun or not? I don't have time to fuck around."

"Nasty little temper you got there, mister big shot. What kind of gun do you want?"

"You mean I have a choice?"

Delilah pushed herself off the desk and said, "This here's a full-service operation...but very expensive."

"How about a Glock 19 and a short-barreled shotgun, preferably a Mossberg?"

For the first time, Delilah smiled, showing a gold front tooth. "I like a man who knows his guns. Come back in an hour and bring me three thousand dollars."

Grant started to protest, but Delilah interrupted, holding up her hand like a traffic cop. "This here ain't no negotiation."

Grant nodded and moved toward the curtain.

Delilah yelled, "Pablo, watch the store," and pulled aside a huge mola to open the back door.

Grant used the hour to get the cash from the hotel safe and find Scammon, who was tasked with finding him a water taxi with an operator who could keep his mouth shut.

When Grant returned to the Internet Café, Delilah again led him through the curtain into the back room, where she opened a small duffel bag and removed a Glock 19 and a Mossberg twelve-gauge pump-action shotgun with a pistol grip. Neither gun was new, but they were oiled and appeared to be in good shape.

Grant inspected the weapons. The Glock held fifteen nine-millimeter rounds in the magazine and one more in the chamber. The Mossberg held seven twelve-gauge rounds with one more in the chamber. Both guns were fully loaded, and she had included a box of ammunition for each weapon.

"No charge for the ammunition and the duffel—on the house. When you're done, I'll buy 'em back for five hunnert dollars. You're not gettin' 'em through the x-ray machine at the airport."

Grant nodded and left through the back door.

CHAPTER 14

Two thousand miles north of Bocas del Toro, Joaquin Archivaldo Guzman Lorea, known as El Chapo (Shorty), ended his conversation with Pedro Martinelli, poured himself two fingers of tequila, and walked across a living room the size of a basketball court, ignoring three bikini-clad women playing cards and two rough-looking men with Glocks in their shoulder holsters. He stood on the veranda of the fifteen thousand-square-foot villa, taking in the commanding view of the ocean in Cabo San Lucas, Mexico. George Clooney was renting a villa down the street, and Jennifer Aniston was staying in the villa below El Chapo's. His proximity to movie stars was purely coincidental; El Chapo didn't stay in one place very long. An associate had rented the villa for a week.

The diminutive fifty-five-year-old Mexican ruled the Sinaloa cartel, allegedly the world's largest and most powerful drug trafficking organization. Every year since 2009, *Forbes* magazine had ranked him one of the world's most powerful people. According to *Forbes*, in 2012 he was the tenth richest man in Mexico, with a net worth of roughly $1 billion USD. Rounding out his claim to fame, the United States offered a $5 million reward for information leading to his capture.

What *Forbes* didn't know would fill volumes. El Chapo ran the Sinaloa cartel under a franchise from the Sanchez family, which had controlled smuggling into the United States from Mexico since the time of Pancho Villa. Carlos Sanchez, the family's most recent patriarch, was dead. One of his sons, Hector, was the president of Mexico. Another son, Ramon, was running the family's day-to-day operations. His only daughter, Boots, was somewhere in southern Texas. El Chapo had been paying the Sanchez family $10 million a month until shortly before Carlos's death. When he stopped paying, Hector unleashed the Mexican Armed Forces and federal police to bring him to heel. El Chapo could have easily continued paying; it wasn't so much the money as being told what to do by anyone, least of all some effete assholes who never got their hands dirty.

Born into a poor family in Sinaloa, rather than going to school, he had sold oranges on the streets to help his family. His father was a small-time opium poppy grower, and El Chapo had used that connection as an introduction to the Sinaloa cartel. He had paid his dues over the years and worked his way up the cartel chain of command to oversee logistics under the tutelage of Miguel "El Padrino" Gallardo. It was only after El Padrino had been arrested and El Chapo had assumed control of the cartel that he learned of the franchise fee to the Sanchez family. Since then he had plotted relentlessly to get out from under the thumb of the Sanchez family and finally saw his chance, as they seemed to be fighting on multiple fronts to keep control of the drug trade. Well-placed bribes were keeping the military and federal police at bay, despite Hector's orders, but that situation could change in a heartbeat if the Sanchezes paid more or, more likely, killed and replaced those who were protecting him.

Within forty-eight hours after Meredith and Chambers had been spotted at Red Frog Beach, El Chapo had a full dossier on them. Meredith was accomplished: a helicopter pilot, an army ranger, founder of BlackRock, and a gringo big hitter.

Meredith had been a thorn in the side of the Sanchez family for several years, but apparently the hatchet had been buried with the death of Carlos. It was just too coincidental that they had showed up in the backwater of Bocas del Toro and went to Red Frog Beach, one of his major transshipment points for cocaine from Peru. The Sanchez family controlled all the cocaine from Colombia, but he had his sources in Peru that were allowing him to circumvent them. It was possible Meredith and Chambers were working with the Sanchezes or maybe even the DEA to get information on his operation.

El Chapo survived in his brutal world by taking no unnecessary chances and refusing to believe in coincidences. He had ordered Chambers kidnapped, figuring she would break before Meredith. Once he wrung everything out of her, she was dead.

Over the years, El Chapo had become a shrewd judge of men, and he knew Meredith would not quit looking for Chambers. He would become a problem unless he was eliminated.

It stood to reason Meredith would get help from BlackRock. It was also logical that the men would not risk an illegal entry into Panama; they would come through the airport like tourists. He had instructed Martinelli to have the police watch the airports and detain the BlackRock operators when they arrived—they surely wouldn't be hard to spot. With any luck they would have weapons in their luggage. He finished by telling Martinelli to have Chambers's kidnappers kill Meredith.

El Chapo looked at the villa below and noticed a woman sunbathing by the pool. He picked up the binoculars and focused on her. Perhaps this was the famous Jennifer Aniston? He had no idea what she looked like, but the woman below was quite attractive—a good body, but not nearly as voluptuous as the women inside who were there to service him as needed. Thinking about his women gave him a tingle in just the right spot. He put down the binoculars and went inside.

The three women put down their cards and looked at him expectantly. Was he going to choose one of them…or maybe all of them?

El Chapo poured himself another drink and pointed at the blonde, who followed him toward his bedroom. She looked back and winked at her compatriots.

CHAPTER 15

Grant sat at a table on the dining deck of the Bocas Hotel with a half-eaten hamburger and an empty bottle of Balboa beer anchoring a map of the Red Frog Beach development. The rental villas were spread out in the jungle about a mile from the public dock, which was the only access point. The jungle was impenetrable except along the fifteen-foot-wide dirt roads; people got around on foot or in golf carts. There was no front desk, lobby, or real estate office on the island. Renters had to arrive before 7:00 p.m. or there would be no one to meet them. He had no way of determining which house was being used by the Mexicans.

There had to be housekeepers, maintenance people, and a few other employees at the development, but Grant had the sense they were day-workers and didn't live in the development. If he went over there and started questioning them, it was highly likely that word would get back to the Mexicans. In fact, the Mexicans probably paid the staff to report any inquiries or other unusual activity concerning them.

He planned to go over there that night, walk from the dock to the house, conduct surveillance, and rescue Stephanie. It was rather straight-forward, except he had no idea which house was the right one. It would be too dangerous and take too much time to go house to house. He had to know which house was the right one.

Grant's free hand rubbed his chin, which hadn't felt a razor since the day Stephanie was kidnapped. His hair wasn't combed, and his eyes were red rimmed. His khaki shorts and rumpled linen shirt had been ready for the laundry several days ago.

"Sorry to say, you're starting to look like you belong here," said Scammon as he pulled out a chair and joined Grant.

"Trust me, I don't. Did you find me a boat and driver?"

"Not yet. I've been giving it a lot of thought, and frankly, I don't think I can help you. Look, Grant, the people here are by and large a decent lot, but they are also cunning. They know the Mexicans are here, and they know they're running drugs. There's no other reason for them to be in Bocas. As worthy as your cause is and as much as you may pay the driver, he could take your money and get more from the Mexicans by selling you out. Suppose you don't tell him where you're going until you're on the water? Once you get there, he'll know that you're not paying a friendly visit and will warn them one way or another. I just don't know any of these guys you could trust."

Grant sat back, picked up his beer bottle, realized it was empty, and put it back down.

"Maybe you could take the panga over yourself?" said Scammon, trying to be helpful.

Grant shook his head. "I could, but I'm going in cold. If someone moved the boat, say, maybe the night watchman at the marina or a lookout, I would be stranded. Trying to get into any of the other boats there would take way too long. To make this work, I have to eliminate as many variables as possible."

Scammon nodded, got up, and went over to the bar and returned with two ice-cold Balboas. "I do have one idea, but you have to think about it carefully. I don't know anything about boats. Back in the last century when I had a lawn, I couldn't even start a lawn mower. But there's Turnbull…"

"For Christ's sake, Scammon, he's a drunk…a loveable one, but a drunk."

Scammon nodded in agreement. "That's true, of course, but he hasn't always been a drunk. A man of your stature has probably heard of Turnbull and Asser, the London tailors who are world famous for their shirts."

Grant nodded.

"That's his family. He was never in that business. His dream was to design and race powerboats offshore. It's a sad story, and that's one of the reasons why he abandoned London society. He designed a Class I powerboat for the Round Britain and Ireland Race. He was supposed to race it but was hospitalized with a horrid case of the flu three days before the race. His younger brother, Harold, who idolized him and was a family favorite, stepped in to race the boat. About an hour out, the boat just disintegrated. Harold was killed, and Peter was completely ostracized. At the funeral, no one would even speak to him. Peter left and turned up here a few years ago, fifty pounds heavier and drowning in booze. I think he would have drunk himself to death by now if it weren't for Delilah."

"That's a sad story. But I don't see how he can help me."

"Sober—even half sober—he could run the boat for you, and you can surely trust him."

"And how do I get him half sober?"

"Delilah."

"And how would she accomplish what would have to be a miracle?"

"There's a lot you don't know about Delilah. Beneath that intimidating exterior and calculating brain is an acolyte of St. Jude. I don't understand it myself, but she actually cares about Turnbull. She makes sure he eats regularly and pays his bills. She's even willing to have sex with him if he's sober. A couple times a month, he sobers up and she beds him. It's all a mystery to me, but get her to sober him up and you'll have a hell of a boat operator."

CHAPTER 16

When Grant pushed open the door of the Internet Café, a dreadlocked, pale-faced boy was holding a fish-fileting knife with a nine-inch blade inches from Delilah's face. The dozen or so other patrons were silently frozen in place. Delilah, standing with her arms raised, looked unperturbed, if slightly annoyed, like a fly had invaded her space.

"I'm not gonna tell you again, fat lady, gimme your money or I'm gonna cut you up."

"Your mother regrets your birth," said Delilah.

A millisecond after uttering those words, Delilah's right hand dropped in a swinging motion and seized the boy's right wrist. Simultaneously, she shifted her body to the left, forcing the knife clear of her body. Pivoting back to the right, her massive left fist collided with his jaw, and the boy slumped to the floor. Delilah casually released the knife from his hand and buried the tip in the counter.

"Pablo, take this idiot to the police," she said.

Grant threaded his way across the room and approached her, smiling. "Quite impressive," he said.

"Shit, my granddaddy done taught hand-to-hand combat tuh special forces during World War Two. He lern't me all his stuff when I was a girl. Comes in handy from time to time. What ken I do fer yuh this time?"

"I'd like to talk to you privately about a few things."

Delilah shrugged. "When Pablo gits back, I'll find yuh down the street on the dock where Turnbull parks his ass when he can't find summon tuh drink wit."

Grant went to the dock and found Turnbull, chin on his chest, gently snoring in his broken lawn chair. Next to the chair was a cooler of Balboas. Grant didn't bother him.

Delilah showed up a few minutes later and pulled two beers out of the cooler. She opened them and handed one to Grant. "He's done had his share fer this afternoon. What yuh wan tuh talk about?"

"No small talk with you, is there, Delilah?"

"My granddaddy always sed, git to the point, girl. Guess it wore off on me."

"I have to ask…how did you end up here?"

Delilah took a long pull of her beer and studied Grant for a moment. "Muh husband was an instructor at the JOTC. I stayed here, and he'd come on weekends when he could. Had his rendezvous with destiny on some secret deployment. Didn't see no reason tuh leave."

Grant nodded. "The tattoo…your husband was in the 101st?"

"Screamin' Eagles Airborne, yeah."

Delilah took another long pull off the beer bottle. "What yuh want?"

"Help. I need someone to operate a boat over to Red Frog Beach. Some Mexicans are staying there, and they may have Stephanie or know where I can find her." Grant pointed at the dozing Turnbull. "Scammon says that sober, he's one hell of a boat operator. I need someone I can trust to get me over there and be there when I finish what I have to do. Scammon says you can sober him up."

Delilah took a sip from the bottle and assessed Grant with narrowed eyes. "Meebe. What's he git out of it?"

"I'll pay, say, five hundred dollars?"

Delilah rolled her eyes and snorted. "Meredith, don take me fer sum fool. Yer goin' over thar wit guns. Yer gunna get yer woman or not; either way, yer gunna cause them Meskins a heap uh grief and then saunter down the hill, step in yer boat, an git the hell outta thar before holy hell comes down on yer hed. An fer all that yer payin' five hunnert? Gimme a break. Me, I'm thinkin' five grand."

Grant took a long pull off his beer, stalling for time. "Can you find out which house the Mexicans are in without alerting them?"

Delilah grinned, and her hard eyes sparkled. "That ken git done, but expensive. Them Meskins are mean mutherfuckers. Doan take no prisoners, if'n you git muh meanin'."

"Okay. How much for all of it?"

"Me, I'm thinkin' seventy-five hunnert sounds 'bout right."

"Done. We leave an hour after dark. Have Turnbull meet me here."

"He'll be here, and he'll know which house. Yuh jest hav thuh cash here."

Delilah walked over and kicked Turnbull's chair. "Come on, git yer fat ass outta that chair. We got work to do."

CHAPTER 17

Grant returned to his hotel, his mind turning over what he didn't know about the Mexicans at Red Frog Beach. Were there only two? Had they been alerted that Grant was on to them? Would there be sentries? Were the women with them? He knew he needed backup—only a fool would go there alone.

Grant dialed Peter Chastain at BlackRock as a solid sheet of tropical rain rolled into Bocas Town with a roar that made it hard to carry on the phone conversation. After Grant explained the current situation, Chastain said BlackRock had ten men training Nicaraguan police that he could move to Panama to help Grant, but they couldn't get to Bocas Town with weapons until the next morning. The company could not risk dropping the men in illegally. If they were caught, it could put the company out of business. They would have to enter the country legally through Tocumen Airport without weapons. To avoid creating a scene at the tiny Bocas Town airport, the men would pick up weapons and other equipment from a black market arms dealer in Panama City and drive all night from Panama City to Almirante, where a private boat would take them to Bocas Town.

Grant needed to think. Should he risk going by himself that night or risk waiting for backup? Anything could happen to Stephanie tonight. If they were aware he was on to them, the Mexicans might leave or move her somewhere else. He opened a beer and sat tilted back in a plastic chair on the small balcony of his hotel, hidden in one of the blue-black shadows cast by the sinking sun. Boats moored in the harbor below bobbed innocently in the slight chop. The humid, salt-laden breeze carried the smell of grilling fish with an undercurrent of rotting garbage.

In reality, this was a military-type decision. The strongest and safest approach was to wait for the BlackRock men. With them, there was little doubt they could take the Mexicans if they were still there. Taking them didn't mean Stephanie would be safe until then or even be in the house. If he went in tonight alone, taking the Mexicans was far from a sure thing. He might even be captured if they were waiting for him. On top of that, he could not be sure Stephanie was even there.

Perhaps there was a middle ground. He could get close enough to watch the house. He could find out if the Mexicans were still there, if Stephanie was with them, and would know if they tried to move her. In essence he would be a scout, a forward observer. It would work as long as he didn't get caught. It would also give him something to do because he couldn't sit still. Once he got Stephanie out of Bocas, he would never set foot in another third-world country unless it was the Little Havana section of Miami.

He and Stephanie had briefly visited Isla Bastimentos. The island was home to the National Marine Park, Bastimentos Town, which the locals called Old Bank, and the Red Frog Beach development, where the Mexicans where staying. The two hundred odd residents of Old Bank were principally African Caribbean descendants from the banana plantation days. The poverty they had seen was both heartbreaking and frightening. There was a collapsed pier, piles of garbage, women playing cards, and men drinking beer or lurking around. He and Stephanie had spent less than ten minutes there.

Red Frog Beach comprised fifteen hundred acres on the twenty-square-mile island. It sported a hurricane-free deepwater marina, where they had counted at least thirty serious ocean-going yachts and a host of smaller boats. They had walked to the beach and back but avoided the rental villas, which were about a mile by dirt road from the public dock. The jungle was virtually impenetrable; he would have to use the road to approach the villas. In the dark, he had no idea what to expect.

Grant called Chastain and filled him in on his decision. Grant was not surprised when Chastain tried to talk him into waiting. When Grant demurred, Chastain suggested he wait at the dock, since that had to be how the Mexicans would leave the island. Grant said he would think about it and that the men should contact Delilah for an update when they got to Bocas Town.

———

Moonlight was glimmering off the water when Grant got to the dock. Delilah was waiting for him, and he handed her an envelope with the money in it. As he moved down the dock, she disappeared.

Turnbull, now in a black watch cap, dark jeans, and a black long-sleeved shirt, was waiting in a sixteen-foot panga. For the first time since he had met Turnbull, there was no odor of alcohol emanating from the man; in fact, he looked alert and slightly excited. Grant stepped down into the boat, and the men shook hands silently.

Turnbull handed Grant a hand-drawn map of the Red Frog Beach development that showed the dock, the path to the clearing from which the dirt roads started, and the road to Villa 24, where the Mexicans were staying. The map also showed a floor plan of the one-story villa and the location of nearby villas.

"Thanks. How does Delilah know Villa 24 is the right one?"

"She asked the daughter of the housekeeper for the villas. Delilah has more contacts in Bocas than anyone."

"It makes sense—it's separated from the others and gives them more privacy," said Grant.

"Delilah thought we might want some of this," said Turnbull, handing Grant a camouflage face-paint kit.

"That woman never ceases to amaze me," said Grant as they covered their faces, necks, and hands in shades of black, green, and brown.

Turnbull merely nodded his agreement before untying the panga and pushing off.

There was no conversation for the twenty-minute trip to Isla Bastimentos and the Red Frog Beach marina. As they rounded the southern point of Isla Bastimentos, a heavy mist enveloped them, diffusing the moonlight and reducing visibility to about twenty yards. Within minutes their clothes were sodden with moisture from the outside and sweat from the inside.

Luxury yachts moored at the marina seemed to rise up out of the mist like ghost ships. Turnbull cut the motor, and they paddled the panga to the floating public dock, where Turnbull expertly tied it to the cleats set in the dock.

Grant motioned him close, gripped his shoulder, and whispered, "Thank you. If I'm not back by dawn, pull out and come in again like a day-tripper and just hang out. If anything happens to compromise your safety, leave and don't look back. I...we can hide in the jungle if necessary and wait for the men to get here. If that doesn't work, I can call you to pick us up."

"If you get hung up, Delilah says there's some kind of a trail through the jungle to Old Bank. I don't know where it is and it's probably pretty dangerous in the dark, but if you're stuck you might be able to find it," whispered Turnbull.

Grant nodded and stepped onto the dock.

Turnbull whispered, "Good luck."

CHAPTER 18

After Grant disappeared into the jungle, Turnbull checked his watch, carefully hoisted his bulk out of the panga, and moved across the dock into the darkness at the jungle's edge to wait. He did it without any particular thought. Something in his subconscious told him to get out of sight.

Of course, there might be a night watchman. Good God almighty, they hadn't discussed the possibility of a watchman. It made sense that there would be one, given all the multimillion-dollar yachts docked here.

As if on cue, a flashlight cut the mist at the far end of the docks—most likely a watchman who might have a weapon. Turnbull had nothing. He didn't know the first thing about fighting. He knelt very slowly and felt around for something he could use as a club. With his luck, he would grab a snake. He stood up slowly and watched the guard making his rounds.

The shadowy figure was moving pretty fast, giving each yacht only a perfunctory once-over with his flashlight as he moved toward the public dock where the panga was tied. The guy was probably bored out of his mind and just going through the motions, but if he saw the panga, he would surely suspect something; it wasn't supposed to be there. Maybe he would think one of the vacationers in the villas or someone camping on the beach had rented it.

Turnbull stood frozen in place, barely breathing, and watched. A cloud of mosquitoes descended upon him. Turnbull gritted his teeth and stood still while they feasted on him.

He held his breath as the watchman moved toward the public dock. He was still a vague outline in the mist, but it seemed to Turnbull that there was a holster on his belt. The man stopped and moved the flashlight across the public dock without going onto it. The panga floated just below the dock's surface; if he stayed where he was, he wouldn't see it. The watchman turned and disappeared back into the mist.

Turnbull began to breathe again. He suddenly had the urge to pee. As he thought about it, the urge became overpowering. He stood close to a tree, unzipped, and unleashed a torrent of urine. The splashing was swallowed by the nighttime rain-forest sounds.

CHAPTER 19

Before Turnbull had left the panga, Grant was lost in the shadows enveloping the path from the dock to the dirt roads. He knelt and removed his backpack, from which he took the Glock 19 and the Mossberg shotgun. There was no need to check his weapons; he had done that in the hotel. Each was fully loaded, with a round in the chamber. He slipped a titanium dive knife with a five-inch blade onto his belt and pushed the Glock under his belt. He stood and moved off, holding the shotgun in front of him. He would scout the house first and then decide whether to act or wait. He told himself it was a sensible plan with minimal risk.

The path led to the clearing in the jungle that served as a hub for the three dirt roads that branched off like spokes in a wheel. Clouds and the heavy mist created an eerie environment with only a few feet of visibility. According to the map he had memorized, the road to Villa 24 was the first one on his left. He moved to the edge of the clearing and started slowly clockwise, waiting for the road to materialize in the mist. The rain forest was alive with sounds—croaking, screeching, and rustling like some unseen presence was slithering toward him. Sweat oozed out of Grant's pores and slid down his skin, turning his damp clothes soggy. There was no breeze in the jungle to keep the gnats and mosquitoes from swarming around him in a cloud. From time to time, he rubbed his face and neck, mashing the mosquitoes into the greasepaint.

The road materialized out of the mist on his left, and he started off down the shoulder, ready to duck into the jungle if anything approached.

One mile to go. The rain forest was a living, breathing organism, masking any noise he might be making.

A faint sound like an electric motor overtook Grant from behind. He ducked off the road and dropped into the jungle as dim lights pierced the mist, moving in his direction. Grant moved farther into the blackness of the jungle and dropped flat. He was sure he couldn't be seen from the road. As he lay there, the sound of voices pierced the night—drunken voices coming closer. Two voices growing louder. They were shouting at each other in German—a man and a woman from the sound of it. It was probably a couple of drunks coming back from a midnight swim or another house to their villa. Grant lay there, waiting for the golf cart to pass. As it vanished into the night, another softer sound took its place—a series of what sounded like farts. What in the hell was it? Stay still or move? He couldn't see anything in the blackness to help him decide. The farting sound continued, maybe two feet to his left. Unable to wait any longer, Grant moved very slowly to stand and felt something strike his left hand. Grant rose to his feet and could feel something hanging from his hand—a snake. He grabbed it behind its head with his right hand and pulled the fangs from his hand. He could feel the snake writhing as he pulled his knife and sliced off its head. Grant carried the snake out to the roadside and turned a penlight on it.

Bad news: it was about eighteen inches long with red and yellow rings. He examined the head, which had short, fixed fangs. A coral snake—poisonous. Good news: its belly was distended from swallowing its dinner not long ago. That was why it hadn't been able to move. Better news, if he was lucky: almost all of its venom had been used to kill its dinner, and there hadn't been enough time for it to rebuild. Best news: a coral snake did not carry much venom in its fangs. It basically delivered its venom by holding on and chewing. This snake hadn't had a chance to chew. Grant threw the snake in the jungle. He knew enough not to cut the bite, which would aid in the spread of the venom. Instead, he cut some material off his shirt-tail and fashioned constricting bands about two inches above the bite and covered the wound with the remaining fabric. He would have to gamble that whatever rodent the snake had killed got most of its venom. In any event, he had some time before other symptoms, if any, set in.

Grant checked the luminous dial on his TAG Heuer Aquaracer: 1:00 a.m.

The road veered to the right and started uphill. As the elevation change dissipated some of the mist, a dark villa materialized out of the gloom on his left. According to the map, this was Villa 17; Villa 24 was perched on a ridgeline overlooking the ocean about a quarter of a mile farther up the road.

The road bent to the left, and there was Villa 24. The mist softened the light coming from the structure, creating the impression the villa was floating in the mist. There was a door on the near side with two regular-sized windows and one smaller one, probably a bathroom. The map showed a small pool on the ocean side of the villa, where he assumed there were big windows to capture the view below.

Nothing seemed to be moving, and he couldn't hear anything. Grant watched for a while. Still nothing. If he moved up to the house, he risked being seen by the Mexicans. However, he didn't know if anyone was there. He was relying on information from Delilah. What if it was wrong? What if the Mexicans were no longer there? He had to find out.

The rain-forest sounds enabled Grant to move quickly to the left side of the villa without being concerned about noise. He bent down by the first window and carefully rose up, peering in from the bottom corner of the window. A bedroom in chaos—sheets and comforter jumbled in the middle of the bed. Women's clothes were strewn everywhere—on the bed, on a chair, on the floor, and spilling out of a dresser. No one was there.

He slipped along the wall to the smaller window. The bathroom was empty. The door had a window, from which he was able to look down a hallway into the living room, which had a huge plate-glass window on the far side.

The rain-forest concert was shattered by laughter and splashing. Female voices, high-pitched Spanish, more laughter, and more splashing—more like a water fight than someone else jumping in the pool.

Grant moved quickly to the last window. Another bedroom, also empty; this one was the opposite of the other one. Bed made and clothes put away, but there was an open, empty suitcase on the bed. The villa had two bedrooms, two and a half baths, and a great room with the living area, kitchen, and dining table. Where could Stephanie be?

He slipped around the side of the villa, moved forward, dropped to his knees, and peered around the corner into the pool area. The two women from Barco Hundido were frolicking in the pool—naked. No one was with them. They were in and out of the pool, jumping off the diving board, and throwing a beach ball around. Neither was particularly tall, but both were voluptuous. Their boobs were obviously real as they bounced around with natural freedom. Where were the men? Was Stephanie here?

Grant went back around to the roadside door and gently opened it. He slipped down the hallway and peered into the great room—empty. He moved quickly through the bedrooms—no sign of the men or Stephanie. No one here but the women. Now what?

If he left, no one would know he had been there. If he questioned the women, they might have some information, but since he had no intention of killing them, they would surely pass on his presence to the Mexicans. Would the information be worth the exposure? Hell, the women might not speak English. He could pretend to be after drugs and not mention Stephanie directly, but there was still the language problem. Could they tell him anything that was worth the exposure? Maybe he could go back to Panama City and track down Martinelli's nephew. No, he was here; maybe his limited Spanish would work.

Grant slipped out the back door, walked around the house, and stood by the pool until the women noticed him. Grant pointed the shotgun at them and in a low, menacing voice said, "Ustedes dos, salir ahora."

The women meekly climbed out of the pool and stood before him, naked, dripping wet, and shaking despite the heat. One was somewhat taller than the other, but beyond that they could have been twins.

"Donde estan sus hombres?"

The women looked at each other, and the shorter one said, "No sabemos, que dejaron."

Grant pointed the shotgun at her stomach and said, "English."

"Gone," said the shorter one.

"Where?" asked Grant, shifting the shotgun toward the shorter one.

They looked at each other again and shrugged. In unaccented English, the taller woman said, "We are *parte niñas*, party girls. They did not tell us where they were going or anything about their business. We are going back to Colombia tomorrow."

Then both women smiled wickedly.

From behind him, Grant heard the unmistakable sound of a shell being racked into a pump-action shotgun.

CHAPTER 20

Grant was moved into the great room and secured to a straight-backed wooden chair with plastic flex-cuffs. His weapons were spread on the dining table. The women were somewhere out of sight. One of the men was on a satellite phone; the other was standing in front of Grant, smoking a thin cigarillo, and staring at him with vacant brown eyes. Both of them were dressed in pressed jeans and polo shirts. Grant recognized the Danner assault boots worn by both. They both had neatly trimmed hair, were physically fit, and showed no signs of recent alcohol or drug use. The way they moved and carried themselves and the way they had acted last night gave them an aura of professionalism. He had no idea whether this was a good or a bad thing. The one thing he did know was that he had to stall for as much time as possible and hope the BlackRock operators would get there in time to rescue him.

The man on the phone wasn't talking much, mostly listening. "Si, Senor Guzman, se hara," said the man with the phone before ending his conversation.

Grant kept his face emotionless as his brain churned. Guzman—head of the Sinaloa cartel. He and Stephanie had really stumbled into the drug world in a big way. He needed to get them talking if he was going to find out anything about Stephanie and run out the clock.

"You guys have names?" asked Grant.

The man in front showed no sign of having heard him. He continued to stare at Grant. The man who had been on the phone came around, stood next to his companion, and said with a smile, "Sure. I'm Marco, and he's Polo."

"Where is Stephanie Chambers?" asked Grant.

"Shut up. We'll be asking the questions, and you'll be answering them," snapped Marco.

Polo reached into his pants pocket and pulled out a clasp knife, which he casually flipped open. He then closed it and put it back in his pocket.

"What would it take for you guys to let me go?"

Polo continued to stare at him. Grant wondered if anyone was home inside his head.

"If you tell us what we want to know, we will probably let you go, but not until then," said Marco, smiling.

"Well, if you want to know what we're doing in Bocas del Toro, I've been asking myself the same question since we got here. We came for a vacation, to get away from it all, but we ended up too far off the grid.

"We didn't know anything about your drug operation here. It didn't come up until you kidnapped Stephanie. Of course, now we know you're here, but so what—there's drug trafficking throughout Latin America. It's not surprising that a Mexican cartel would have operations in Panama. If I'd thought about it before we came, I would have assumed you had a presence here. So there are no surprises. Actually, I couldn't care less about you and your drugs. I'm not law enforcement, and I don't work for the government. If it were up to me, I would legalize drugs; so I'm not a crusader either. Bottom line, just let us go, and we can all carry on as before. Stephanie and I will be out of Panama as fast as humanly possible, and we'll write all this off as another bad chapter in a horrible vacation."

Polo remained expressionless. Marco smiled. "As you wish." Then he nodded to Polo, who retrieved his knife and flipped it open with an audible click.

Grant looked at the knife and then up at Marco. "Marco, you know I'm telling the truth because it makes sense. If you torture me, I'm not much different from anyone else. Sooner or later I'll tell you anything to get you to stop. Polo here might enjoy a little knife work, but it won't get you any closer to the truth, which I have already told you."

Marco put one hand on his chin with the other holding his elbow and cocked his head slightly to the left. He looked carefully at Grant, as if he were studying a rare painting. Finally, he sighed and dropped his arms.

"A sad story and probably true, so I'll believe you. However, unfortunately for you, we have our orders," said Marco.

"You said you would let us go."

"I lied."

Still no expression on Polo's face. He stood perfectly still with the knife in his hand.

"Look, Marco, for an obviously well-educated man, I don't think you understand. I'm something of a public figure in the United States. If you kill me, it won't be just another drug killing; it will unleash the full power of the US government on your organization. You and your boss will regret such a rash action."

"Well, thank you for the compliment, Mr. Grant Meredith, head of BlackRock. We know who you are, and frankly—and I know this will come as a surprise—we don't care. El Chapo intends to teach you people a lesson. If you come after him, there will be severe personal consequences. You are fighting an impossible battle—your people, people everywhere, want drugs, and they are going to get them from us or someone else.

"We aren't going to make you disappear, Mr. Grant Meredith; we're going to make an example of you. Think of it this way: your death may serve a useful purpose."

A few minutes later, as Marco hustled the women out of the house with their suitcases, he nodded to Polo and said, "Voy a tomar estas bellezas al muelo. Suavizar Meredith mientras yo me haya ido, pero quiero que funcione cuando vuelva."

Polo watched Marco and the women leave in a golf cart before turning to Grant. Almost to himself, he said, "Ahora me pertences."

Grant only caught a few words, but it looked like he was in for a session with Polo.

CHAPTER 21

Stephanie paced back and forth on the twenty-by-fifteen-foot deck that fronted a similar-sized living area with a small bathroom jutting off the back. From time to time, she dropped to the deck and did push-ups, sit-ups, and stretching exercises—anything to keep the rage inside her in check. She was in a cage from which escape seemed impossible.

Another damnable over-the-water bungalow, similar to the one she had shared with Grant, but with several major differences. This one was completely enclosed in heavy wire mesh, like that used to form concrete. There was only one securely locked, reinforced door opening onto a short walkway that ended in an impenetrable jungle. No other structures were in sight. Worst of all, her cage was in a small inlet, offering no view to the ocean. She could see the overgrown ten-foot opening in the jungle that was a water passage to the ocean. She could close the side windows, but the front deck was an open cage. There was a cot, a table, and a chair. She had a towel, clean jeans, and a T-shirt. There was food and water in the cupboard but no refrigerator, stove, or electricity. Thus far, her diet had consisted of peanut butter sandwiches, dried fruit, and water. For variety, there was lettuce and tomato. No silverware; she spread the peanut butter with her finger.

The isolation was complete. It was her own fault; her own stupidity had gotten her into this mess. Her decision had been made in a split second, and it had been a mistake. The men who had approached her table had told her that three other men were waiting for Grant outside the men's room and would kill him if she didn't come with them. They had said they just wanted to ask her a few questions in private. They would simply move the water taxi a short distance from the dock, and she would be back for desert. She wasn't naïve, but if they weren't lying, Grant would be taken by surprise; he wouldn't have a chance. If she went with them, she would have a chance—probably not much of one, but a chance.

Out on the water, just past the boats moored in the harbor, the men had cut the engine and they had drifted. The leader had looked to be about thirty and had a face that was a mess. The right side was normal, almost handsome, but the left was hideously scarred, and his left ear was missing along with two fingers on his left hand. He had been dressed in expensive dark slacks and a white guayabera shirt. As he politely but pointedly had asked her questions about Red Frog Beach, he had kept his head turned to minimize her view of his scarred face. Why were she and Grant there? What were they looking for? Had they boarded any of the boats? Where had they gone? Why weren't they staying longer?

This had gone on for about ten minutes. The other men in the water taxi were rough looking, probably Mexican. It hadn't taken long for Stephanie to surmise that these were drug traffickers who used the marina at Red Frog Beach to move drugs.

Most disconcerting had been her questioner's use of Grant's name; he also had referred to her as Ms. Chambers. She and Grant had once again stumbled into the drug trade.

The young man had finally run out of questions and had used a satellite phone to make a call. He had moved to the bow of the water taxi, turned away from her, and spoken softly in Spanish. Stephanie spoke Spanish but could hear only part of his end of the conversation.

"I don't think so…yes…yes…Are you sure…No, no, I understand… As you wish."

Then he had turned to her and said, "Thank you for your co-operation, Ms. Chambers. We will take you back for desert."

The motor had started, and the boat had turned back toward the restaurant. Stephanie had relaxed just a bit before something slammed into the side of her head, knocking her off the bench and onto the bottom of the boat. She had still been conscious as her mouth had been roughly covered with duct tape, a cloth bag that smelled of ether had been forced over her head, and her wrists had been jerked behind her and secured with plastic flex-cuffs. She had fought to stay awake, but the blow to her head, the ether smell, and the rocking of the boat soon put her to sleep.

———

If she could do it again, she would call their bluff and raise holy hell, making as much noise as she could to warn Grant. At least they would have gone down fighting. Maybe they got Grant anyway. She didn't know.

Stephanie dropped and did fifty push-ups. She had to calm down and keep it together. She had surveyed every inch of the wire mesh—there were no weaknesses. Even the ceiling was covered with the mesh. She felt like a caged animal.

Stay calm. Someone would come sometime; they weren't going to starve her to death. She had to be ready. She needed a plan.

CHAPTER 22

There was no expression on Polo's face as he tested the blade of his knife with a calloused thumb. Marco and Polo were competent professionals, but they had made two mistakes: they had not tied Grant's legs to the chair, and they had underestimated him.

Polo moved toward him, and when he was a stride away, Grant lunged forward, driving his head upward into the underside of Polo's chin. Polo's head snapped back, and they fell in a heap with Grant on top. He struggled to his feet, keeping an eye on Polo, who lay motionless.

Grant moved to the kitchen island, held the seat of the chair away from his back, and pivoted hard into the counter. The chair broke apart, leaving Grant's wrists cuffed to the chair back. He sat on the floor and maneuvered his hands under his rear end and feet, getting his hands in front of him. The next step was to pick up Polo's knife and cut the flex-cuffs from his hands.

Polo was still out cold. Grant didn't speak enough Spanish, and, to his knowledge, Polo didn't speak any English, so he wasn't going to be interrogating the Mexican. Maybe one of the men coming from BlackRock spoke Spanish, so the question was whether to leave Polo here or take him to the dock. Best to leave him here—he would just be in the way, and Grant had to focus on Marco and the women. Grant found some flex-cuffs on the table next to his guns and, using three pairs, secured Polo's hands and feet and then folded his legs back and looped the last pair over the cuffs, securing his hands and ankles. He wasn't going anywhere.

Grant picked up his weapons and backpack and looked around the house and grounds. There were no more golf carts—only an old bicycle. It had been years since Grant had ridden a bike. He pulled on the backpack, which now held the weapons, and grabbed the handlebars with his left hand to pull the bike around; it slipped out of his hand and fell to the ground. Grant looked at his forearm in surprise—the skin surrounding the bite was an angry red, with duller red streaks spreading up and down his arm. Grant shook his hand and flexed his fingers. They worked but without much strength.

There wasn't anything he could do about the bite now; he had to surprise Marco at the dock. Maybe, if his luck changed, the men from Blackrock had already stopped Marco. If they weren't there, Turnbull would be in danger. Grant picked up the bike with his right hand and, after a wobbly start, took off for the dock.

———

The sun was inching above the horizon into a clear sky without even a hint of a breeze. The sea air was heating quickly. Turnbull was sweating profusely but not from the rising heat. Where in the hell was Meredith? Maybe he was dead and Turnbull was waiting for a corpse. Maybe he would show up running full speed with the Mexicans in hot pursuit. Why hadn't he brought a gun from Delilah's small arsenal?

After the watchman had passed, Turnbull had spent the rest of the night at the edge of the jungle, waiting. Just before dawn, he had quietly paddled about a quarter mile from the dock, turned around, started the motor, and returned to the dock as if having just arrived. The watchman roused himself and watched Turnbull tie up to the public dock and then began fueling a water taxi.

Where in the hell were the men from BlackRock? They should be here by now. Very faintly in the distance, Turnbull heard a motor—maybe it was them. As the panga drew into view, he could see there was only one person aboard. No help there.

Turnbull couldn't help himself—he started down the dock toward the dirt path that disappeared into the jungle. Just as he got to the end of the dock, an electric golf cart barreled into sight carrying a man and two women. As they got closer, he could see the man looked like one of the Mexicans Grant had described. The women were flashy—certainly not from Bocas. What had happened to Grant?

The Mexican waved him out of the way and continued down the dock to the watchman's shack. The watchman, who had finished fueling the water taxi, leaped onto the dock when he saw the golf cart coming. He helped the women into the boat and took off immediately. The Mexican turned the golf cart around and came back down the dock.

Turnbull was frozen in place. What was he supposed to do?

———

Grant coasted to a stop just before the dirt path opened toward the dock. He pushed the bike into the jungle and pulled off his backpack. No need to hide his weapons now; the Glock went into his belt in front of his belly button, and the Mossberg rested easily in his hands as he moved around the bend and hugged the jungle while observing the dock. Turnbull was between him and the golf cart, which was heading toward Turnbull.

Marco stopped next to Turnbull and stepped out of the golf cart with a big .45 automatic in his hand.

"Get in, fat man, you're driving," said Marco, waving the pistol.

Grant stepped back into the jungle. As the cart passed, he stepped out and clubbed Marco with the Mossberg on the side of his head. Startled, Turnbull stopped the cart and looked back at Grant, who grabbed Marco by the collar and pulled him from the cart.

"Have you got anything to tie him up?" asked Grant.

"No, but there may be something on the panga or on another boat."

Grant and Turnbull wrestled Marco's inert body into the back of the golf cart, spun around, and headed back to the dock. When they got to the panga, they found nothing but the line tying the boat to the dock.

"Let's check the other boats. There has to be something," said Grant. They frantically searched for rope or anything with which to tie Marco. It took them a couple minutes before they found some rope on a boat half-way down the dock.

They hustled back to the golf cart together. Just before they got to the cart, Marco sat up and pointed the Mossberg shotgun at them.

Marco shook his head slightly as if to clear the cobwebs as he climbed out of the cart and stood five feet in front of them.

"You," said Marco, pointing the shotgun at Turnbull, "tie his hands behind him. Tight."

Grant turned, and Turnbull ran the rope around Grant's wrists and tied it with a loose half hitch.

Marco roughly pushed Turnbull away and jerked the knot tighter. Then he turned and faced Turnbull, raising the Mossberg. "You, I don't need—"

Marco's head exploded in a shower of red mist.

Turnbull and Grant both dropped to the deck and looked around.

"What...ha...ha...happened?" asked Turnbull.

"No idea," whispered Grant. "Slide over here and untie me."

As Turnbull pulled the knot loose, they heard the roar of an outboard motor approaching the public dock. The motor died, and they saw a man leap from a panga, carrying a rifle with a huge telescopic sight. He slipped a looped tie line on the dock cleat.

Grant was scrambling for a gun when the man shouted, "Are you all right?"

"Grant, its Pablo, from the Internet Café," shouted Turnbull.

"Did you shoot him?" asked Grant as he jumped to his feet.

"Yeah, it looked like he had it in for Turnbull here."

"What are you doing here?" asked Turnbull.

"Where were you?" asked Grant.

"Slow down, guys," said Pablo. "I was about a hundred yards out. Delilah sent me. The BlackRock guys were detained at Tocumen Airport, and she thought you might need some help."

"I owe you my life, Pablo. That guy was going to kill me," said Turnbull, rushing as if he were out of breath.

"Glad I got here in time," said Pablo.

"Where did you learn to shoot like that?" asked Grant.

"I served with Delilah's husband at the JOTC; he was the E7 on a lot of missions where I was a sniper. When he went on that last mission, I told him that if he didn't make it back, I would keep an eye on her, be sure she was safe. He didn't, and I have. Anyway, I left the army and needed a job. She needed someone to help out at the café, so it works out pretty good."

"Well, I'm glad you still have your skills," said Turnbull, reaching out to shake Pablo's hand.

"Okay, guys, let's get this body in our panga and wash off the dock. We can tie some weight to him and drop the body in the ocean on the way back."

"Pablo, I hope you speak Spanish," said Grant.

"Si, señor," quipped Pablo.

"Good. Turnbull, you had better stay here and keep an eye on things. It could be a problem if some day-trippers from Bocas dock here and see the body."

CHAPTER 23

Grant and Pablo found Polo where Grant had left him. Grant used Polo's knife to cut the flex-cuff that held his arms and legs together. Together, Grant and Pablo lifted Polo and dropped him on the sofa.

For ten minutes Pablo said nothing, simply ignoring the questions Pablo fired at him in rapid Spanish. Exasperated, Grant picked up Polo's knife and said to Pablo, "Tell this son of a bitch that if he doesn't tell me where Stephanie is being held, I'm going to start cutting off body parts."

Polo straightened up as best he could and said in perfect English, "All right, I'll tell you if you give me a cigarette first; I have one left in the pack in my shirt pocket."

Grant nodded, and Pablo pulled out the pack, stuck the filtered cigarette in Polo's mouth, and lit it. Polo promptly bit off the filter, swallowed it, and smiled.

"Shit," yelled Grant, recognizing what had happened. "It's a suicide pill. We've got to make him throw up."

They tried the Heimlich maneuver, pushed on his stomach, and stuck a spoon down his throat. Nothing worked. Four minutes from the time he swallowed the filter, Pablo began to violently convulse; then he slumped over and his eyes closed. Two minutes later he was dead.

"Shit, shit," said Grant, pounding his leg. "Who would have thought he would have a potassium cyanide pill? This isn't some fucking spy movie."

"There was no way we could have known. You can't blame yourself. Shit happens," whispered Pablo.

Grant stood up and began pacing the room, stopping every few feet and cursing. "We have zip, nada, nothing. They've had Stephanie for three days. Christ, we don't even know if she's alive. Goddamn it!"

———

Grant sent Turnbull back to Bocas with Pablo. He didn't want anyone else involved in dumping the bodies, which he dropped overboard outside the normal channel between Bocas Town and Red Frog Beach.

The decision to dump the bodies rather than get involved with the police sent Grant across the line for the first time. He had always played by the rules, colored inside the lines, but this time he had crossed over without a second thought. He just didn't want to get involved with the local police. He didn't have time; he had to find Stephanie. Finding her had become a mission that he was going to accomplish no matter what. If she was dead, he was going to find El Chapo and kill him. Blow off his fucking head.

As Grant redirected his panga toward Bocas Town, blinding sunlight poured down from above and reflected off the water, making it difficult to see without a hat or sunglasses. He had washed off the face paint with seawater, leaving his face tight with salt and sun. More uncomfortable than the sun was a nagging feeling that he was the only one who had been surprised at Red Frog Beach. His capture had gone down smoothly, like the Mexicans had been waiting for him, using the naked women as bait. How had they known he was coming and when he would be there? Then there was the detention of the BlackRock contingent. The more he thought about it, the more it felt like he had been lured into a trap. Why had the Mexicans exposed themselves so soon after taking Stephanie by going to Barco Hundido? Had they known he would be there? Had he been set up by someone? The Valley Girl, Turnbull, Scammon, Delilah, the maid, or her daughter…it was a troublesome list. Nevertheless, he had to trust someone, but he would be very careful about sharing information unless it was absolutely necessary.

Back at his hotel in Bocas Town, he called Chastain at BlackRock. One of the men detained at Tocumen Airport spoke Spanish and overheard the customs officials refer to Pedro Martinelli as the source of the order to hold the men. It was a good move. Someone had been thinking ahead when Stephanie had been taken—someone who knew who he was. Maybe it was Martinelli, but more probably El Chapo had told Martinelli to be on the lookout for BlackRock personnel coming to help Grant. They couldn't help him now, so he sent them back to Costa Rica.

Martinelli was the only one of Stephanie's captors left. He was going to have to go after Pedro Martinelli, the nephew of the president of Panama. On the brighter side, if there was one, Martinelli would be easier to find than El Chapo, his only other lead.

The only good news was his arm. The red marks going up his arm had faded, and most of the feeling had returned to his left hand. The bite itself was still red, but more like a minor infection—something to be thankful for.

CHAPTER 24

Grant spent the night tossing and turning, waiting for morning. He knew he needed sleep, but it wouldn't come. Too much time was passing. How much time did they need to interrogate Stephanie? It could all be over already. His only remaining lead was Martinelli, and that meant Panama City.

When Grant arrived at the Internet Café, he was directed to the waterfront construction site across the street. There were no workers in sight, but the gate was open, so Grant picked his way through the construction debris to the dock, which looked to be in good shape. He found Turnbull and Delilah sitting in plastic chairs drinking coffee from Styrofoam cups. They nodded hello to one another. There was a chair waiting for him, with a cup of coffee in the seat. Grant picked up the coffee, pulled off the lid, and joined them.

Could either or both of them have set him up for the Mexicans? Marco had been going to kill Turnbull, which argued against his involvement, but on the other hand, maybe Marco considered Turnbull a loose end or he didn't want to pay him. Delilah? Maybe she would sell him out for money, but if she had done that, she probably wouldn't have let Turnbull go into harm's way. Time to play it by ear.

"Nice view. I have to ask...what's in your cup, Turnbull?"

Turnbull grinned. "Straight coffee. Beer is my usual breakfast drink, but it doesn't seem necessary now that I'm sober. A most unusual occurrence, I must admit."

Delilah punched Turnbull's arm playfully. "Sumpin' happened to him las night. This mornin' he tole me he was goin' on the wagon. Heard bull like this before, but this time he seems serious. Mighten even last a day or two."

"Good for you, Turnbull," said Grant.

"What's the plan?" asked Turnbull.

"I think we were set up last night. The Mexicans were waiting for me at the house. Any idea how that might have happened?" asked Grant, looking back and forth between Turnbull and Delilah.

Turnbull looked genuinely shocked. Delilah sat back in her chair, obviously thinking.

Grant waited as the silence lingered long enough to become uncomfortable. Turnbull started to break the silence, but Delilah held up her hand to stop him.

Finally, Delilah sat forward and spoke. "The first thing you can do is cross me and Turnbull ofen yer list. Scammon is possible but unlikely. How would he contact them? We've been around him for quite a while and he's jes not the type. If'n I was tuh go along with your assumption 'bout bein' set up, most likely candidate is the maid because sheez over at Red Frog Beach and could easily come into contact wit dem while cleanin' thur house. That said, they could jes as easily have had summon pullin' sentry duty that saw you arrive. Turnbull said there was a watchman on the dock...mebee he dimed yuh. Maid or sentry, don make no difference now. They's all gone, and neither of them wud know whar yur woman is."

Grant sipped his coffee, considering Delilah's analysis. It made sense that the most likely way they knew he was coming that night was either the maid or the watchman. He had to trust someone, and neither Turnbull nor Delilah seemed the type to sell him out.

"You're probably right, Delilah. And like you say, it doesn't matter now. The job is to find Stephanie. She wasn't kidnapped for ransom. The Mexicans are running drugs through here, and Red Frog Beach is a transshipment point. It's perfect—an isolated deepwater port in a hurricane-free area. Ocean-going yachts owned by people from all over Latin America coming and going. We went over there one day, and the Mexicans want to know what we're up to. They'll have a hard time believing it's just a coincidence," said Grant.

"So you think they'll let her go?" asked Turnbull.

Delilah snorted derisively.

"No. It's less dangerous for them if they just tie some weight to her ankles and drop her in the ocean. No one to identify them," said Grant.

Turnbull and Delilah had nothing to say. The humidity had become a wet blanket of reality.

"Look," said Grant. "Martinelli is the best link we have left. I'm going to Panama City to have a private conversation with him."

"I'll go with you," said Turnbull eagerly. "Watch your back."

Grant looked at Turnbull carefully. His eyes were bright. He had moved to the edge of his chair, full of energy and ready to go. Sober, he could be useful in Bocas Town.

"Thanks, Turnbull, but I think you would be more valuable here. It could still be a kidnapping for ransom, and someone could leave a demand at the hotel while I'm gone. I'm keeping my room, and you could keep an eye on it. Maybe get the hotel staff to let you know if anyone comes around asking for me or leaves a note or something for me. You could ask around about anything unusual that might tie to Stephanie, and you would be here if I needed you to do something. Anyway, I won't be gone long. I know they could have taken her anywhere, but I think she's somewhere in Bocas. The further they moved her, the more likely someone would notice."

Turnbull sat quietly, mulling it over. He looked at Delilah.

"He's right," she said. "Yuh wud be more useful here. How much you payin'?"

"Quiet, Delilah," snapped Turnbull. "It's the right thing to do."

Delilah rocked back in her chair like she'd been slapped. She looked carefully at Turnbull like she hadn't really seen him in a long time.

After a pause she said, "Yur call."

"How long will it take to drive to Panama City?" asked Grant.

"Hard to do," said Delilah. "First, yuh catch a ferry from here to Altamira—takes about two hours. Then yuh got a ten- or twelve-hour drive on tough roads, and yuh need a car, which can be hard to come by."

Grant stared at the homes across the harbor and processed the information. "Too long. But if I fly, I can't take my weapons."

Turnbull looked at Delilah.

"Well, I has a fren who used to pal wit my old man at the JOTC thar at Fort Sheridan. He stuck around afta the base was giv'n to Panama in 1999. I spect he could fix yuh up, but it wouldn't be no charity deal. Cash. That would be the only way fer him."

"Call him," said Grant, standing, "and let me know. I'll get the noon plane."

Delilah provided Grant with a picture of Pedro Martinelli she had copied off the Internet and suggested he might start looking for Martinelli at the presidential palace in the Casco Viejo area of Panama City.

CHAPTER 25

When El Chapo's satellite phone rang, he was in bed with two of his women, sated from several hours of acrobatic sex. A combination of Viagra and plenty of tequila had kept him going. In fact, he had not ejaculated, but it had been pleasurable nonetheless. He was staring languidly at the western sky, where a few low-hanging clouds created a magnificent sunset. Irritated by the ring tone, he untangled himself and walked naked onto the veranda of the massive bedroom, where he stood stone-faced, holding his phone and listening. The only sign of emotion was in his knuckles, which were white from gripping the telephone.

Two of his best men missing and presumed dead. The Colombian women confirmed that his men had captured Meredith. Martinelli confirmed that the men from BlackRock had been successfully detained at the airport. Meredith had done this by himself. The man was loose, possibly jeopardizing his entire Panama operation.

He instructed the caller to send a team of five sicarios from Sinaloa to Bocas Town to dispose of Meredith. No more subtlety—just blow him away as soon as they saw him.

CHAPTER 26

A thin layer of clouds diffused the light from a rising moon as Stephanie sat motionless in the lotus position, back straight, feet on thighs A thin sheen of perspiration covered her body, but she was oblivious to the humidity that earlier she thought could be cut with a knife. She was clad in only her panties, and her meditation allowed a brief respite from her surroundings. The sound of an approaching outboard motor snapped her back to reality. Slowly placing her feet on the floor and keeping her back straight, she rose to a standing position.

A panga with three people on board nosed through the mangroves from the ocean. Stephanie watched the panga approach her cage as she toweled off and pulled on jeans and a T-shirt.

As the panga nudged the dock, the man standing in the bow seemed to float onto the dock, where he quickly secured the boat. It was too dark to see the men clearly until one of them turned on a battery-powered lantern. Even then, their faces were in the shadows.

The taller shadow led the men to her wire-mesh door.

"Ms. Chambers, please turn the chair away from the door and sit in it. We are coming in," said the lead man in a calm voice with an unmistakable Australian accent.

When Stephanie hesitated, he said in a tone that indicated he was used to being obeyed, "Do it now. If you don't, we will put you in the chair, and it will be an unpleasant experience that you could have easily avoided."

Stephanie's mind raced through her options. Could she outfight these men and win? Probably not; they likely had guns and knives. There was no point in giving them an excuse to beat her. Bottom line: she wasn't prepared to take them on...for now.

Without any real choice, Stephanie turned the straight-backed wooden chair away from the door and sat. She heard the metal-on-metal sound of the door being unlocked and the footsteps moving into the room. Her arms were quickly and efficiently pulled behind her, tied, and secured to the chair. Next, her legs were likewise secured to the chair. The snug bonds felt like the coated ropes used on boats. She could not move her wrists or ankles, but she was not tied so tightly as to be painful.

The three men moved in front of her, and the taller man put the lantern on the floor off to the side, casting the men in an eerie, dull light. The man standing closest to her was obviously the leader. The other two men stood on either side, several steps behind him.

The man in front of her appeared to be in his midthirties. Short hair, a weather-beaten face, and a ramrod-straight posture screamed ex-military. He was dressed in boat shoes with no socks, faded jeans, and a tight polo shirt that emphasized a well-developed physique.

The men behind him were a different story altogether. With shaved heads and dressed in only shorts and sandals, they were covered in hideous tattoos from the tops of their heads to their ankles. One of them appeared to have a glass eye.

Stephanie was still trying to absorb the scene before her when the man in front of her smiled and spoke.

"Ms. Chambers, you may call me James or Mr. Bond. Names don't really matter, but they facilitate conversation, and we are going to have a conversation about you and Mr. Meredith. My employer is most anxious to know who you are working for or with and what you are doing in a backwater like Bocas del Toro and, most especially, Red Frog Beach."

Stephanie started to speak, but he held up his hand.

"Don't speak until I ask you to. I think it best that you understand your situation before you say anything. I have a great deal of experience interrogating people; in fact, that's what I did for the army and now do for a living in the civilian world. If I think you are telling me the truth, this experience will not be exceedingly painful, but if I think you are lying to me or not being completely forthcoming, well, that is why my friends from MS-13 are here."

Stephanie glanced involuntarily at the tattooed men. With their lips pulled back exposing jagged, yellow teeth, they looked like they were awaiting a human sacrifice. As they stood there, the rancid odor of unbathed flesh combined with testosterone slowly enveloped her.

The man calling himself Bond watched her watching his companions.

"Yes, they are somewhat intimidating, aren't they? Most people talk right away and tell us what they think we want to hear. That always ends in a painful interlude before they tell us what we want to know. There is a difference, you see."

The self-styled James Bond reached out and touched Stephanie's cheek. His fingers were calloused—rough as sandpaper.

"According to the file I have reviewed, you were a CIA assassin. That is quite impressive; not because you have killed people, but because you must be very intelligent. You were probably trained to defeat a lie detector test. Therefore, you are probably thinking if you can fool the machine, you can fool me. I understand that…but you can't."

Stephanie started to speak again, and Bond slapped her across the mouth, drawing blood that left a metallic taste in her mouth.

"As I said before, do not speak until I ask you to. I expect you to obey me."

Stephanie knew better, but she couldn't help herself. She spit blood at him.

Bond raised his eyebrows, sighed, and said, "Cholo, right little finger, if you please."

The man with the glass eye walked behind her, bringing with him the cloud of body odor and testosterone. He grabbed her little finger and bent it back until it snapped, making an audible sound. Stephanie swallowed the pain, but a tear leaked from the corner of her left eye.

The man went back to his place, and through misty eyes, she saw a smirk tugging at the corners of his mouth.

"That is how it goes when you don't obey. Do not speak, but nod if you understand, Ms. Chambers."

The pain from her finger was shooting up her arm. She nodded.

"Now, you probably think you can hold out until Mr. Meredith or someone else rescues you. That is a thought you must banish from your consciousness because it will not happen. This is most assuredly not a motion picture. The leadership of the local and national police are beneficiaries of our largess, and Mr. Meredith, well...I understand he is enjoying his last hours on Earth as we speak. To survive, you must do what I ask, am I clear?"

Stephanie nodded.

"Good. I want to make sure that you understand what I mean by obey. Cholo, come here."

The man with the glass eye moved beside Bond.

"Show her your package."

Cholo pulled down his shorts, exposing a flaccid penis covered with inflamed red warts over the tattoo of a snake.

For the second time, Stephanie couldn't help herself; she looked, winced, and closed her eyes.

Bond slapped her again and spoke as he would to a naughty child. "When we return, you will suck his dick. Then I will be ready to begin our conversation. If you don't, well...I can assure you that within a very short period of time, you will beg him to put his dick in your mouth."

They untied her, ordered her to remain in her chair until they were gone, and left. The metallic sound of the door closing filled the emptiness.

CHAPTER 27

Grant arrived at tiny Albrook Airport in Panama City with only a small carry-on bag. He didn't plan on staying very long. As he entered the terminal, he saw a tall bald man wearing dark sunglasses looming over the arriving passengers. The man nodded his head. Delilah's contact.

The bald man introduced himself as Bob Edgar. Dressed in an immaculate black suit and crisp white shirt and tie, he didn't look like someone who would be doing Delilah favors. Edgar efficiently ushered Grant into his car, a shiny black BMW 750Li, which was parked just outside the terminal, and they joined the flow of traffic into the city.

Edgar deftly lit a cigarette with an old Zippo lighter encrusted with the 101st Airborne logo.

"Were you with the 101st?" asked Grant in an effort to get a conversation started.

"Thirty years, six months, and twenty-five days. Spent nine years here at the JOTC until it closed in '99," responded Edgar in a deep voice that reminded Grant of a drill sergeant.

"Why the suit and tie in this climate?" asked Grant.

"I'm head of security at the Trump Ocean Club downtown. Got to look official. Just another uniform to me."

"Must be a good place to work."

Edgar turned to look at Grant. Grant saw himself reflected in Edgar's mirrored sunglasses.

"Look, Meredith, I don't have a lot of time to shoot the shit with you. Delilah told me about your woman being kidnapped and that you want a sidearm while you are here."

"Okay, yeah, I need a weapon. Some very unpleasant people have taken Stephanie."

Edgar abruptly turned down a quiet treelined street and pulled to the curb, turned off the engine, and twisted in the seat to face Grant, one arm on the steering wheel and the other on the back of his seat. Heat and humidity immediately oozed into the car.

"Unpleasant people?" snapped Edgar, leaning toward Grant. "You are talking about drug-dealing Mexicans, Meredith. The ones they send here are the cream of the crop, not Juarez gangbangers. They are smart and good at what they do, especially killing without hesitation if their business is threatened. It's no state secret that Pedro Martinelli is aligned with them and sells them protection from the government."

Grant, in no mood to be lectured by a stranger, twisted in his seat to face Edgar.

"Tell me something I don't know. I don't need lectures; I need a gun. Have you got one or not? And take of those sunglasses. Are you trying to pretend you're some kind of junior G-man?"

The cords in Edgar's neck stood out like steel cables; his right shoulder shifted like he was going to hit Grant. Then he relaxed but didn't take off the sunglasses.

"Okay, look, Meredith, I apologize. I'm trying to help. Delilah's old man took a bullet for me during a firefight. Saved my life. Promised I'd look after her if anything happened to him. She is more than capable of taking care of herself, but I owe him and now her. That's the way it is. Keep your cool and listen for a minute. I've got a sidearm for you, but I don't think you want it.

"I know you're familiar with the situation in Mexico. It's not as bad here because we don't have a border with the US, but there is plenty of corruption in the security services and the judiciary. There's just too much money floating around. The temptation is too great. Not all of them are corrupt by any means, but if you get caught up with the wrong cops and the wrong judge, you'll end up dead or in a jail cell for a very long time. Pedro Martinelli arranges things for the Mexican cartels—he makes the payoffs after taking a healthy commission. If his people get ahold of you, it will go very badly. If you get caught with a sidearm, they'll probably shoot you, fire your weapon, put it in your dead hand, and claim self-defense. End of story. If you feel naked without a weapon, pick up a knife at any sporting goods store."

Grant looked out the window and digested the warning. After almost a minute, he nodded and turned back to Edgar.

"Okay. That's good advice. What can you tell me about Martinelli?"

"Single, about thirty; short, five foot five or so; wears boots with thick soles and heels to make him seem taller. Usually moves around with two bodyguards from the national police. Most pictures of him are airbrushed to hide the scars on the left side of his face and a missing left ear, caused by an explosion cooking meth when he was a teenager. Lives in Casco Viejo, has an office in the presidential palace. He comes to the Ocean Club from time to time, usually with a hooker. Best judgment: an insecure snake of the poisonous variety."

Grant nodded to himself, and Edgar started the car.

Edgar dropped Grant at the Canal House, a small hotel in Casco Viejo. They shook hands. There was nothing more to say.

CHAPTER 28

Grant had read about Casco Viejo in travel magazines when he had been planning the trip. The oldest part of Panama City, it had been built on a narrow one-hundred-acre peninsula, making it easy to defend against pirates. Now the old city overlooked the Pacific entrance to the Panama Canal. Across the bay, on Punta Paitilla, the skyline was choked with new high-rise buildings worthy of Singapore.

Casco's narrow streets were a kaleidoscope of seventeenth- and eighteenth-century buildings. Some were ruins, sprouting palm trees visible through window openings; others were crumbling pastel structures housing the impoverished. Nets covered the façades of those being renovated, and many of the three-story buildings were beautifully restored with flower-filled hanging balconies. The overall effect combined Havana and New Orleans spiced with just enough danger to make it interesting for tourists in the daytime and young people in search of its nightlife.

Grant checked into the three-room hotel, which, according to a plaque in his room, had hosted Daniel Craig during the filming of *Quantum of Solace* and set out on foot to scout the presidential place or El Palacio de las Garzas, the Palace of the Herons. On the way he stopped to buy a cheap camera and a Panama hat, made in Ecuador as they all were, to go with the street map he had taken from the hotel.

Shortly before reaching the palace, he noticed several young men in dark suits loitering on corners and in doorways, scrutinizing passersby from behind dark glasses. Earpieces with cords running under their jackets marked them as security service personnel. As he approached the beautiful Spanish colonial palace, which sat on a cordoned-off street over-looking the Bay of Panama, the security became more obvious. Scores of men in SWAT-type uniforms with automatic weapons were on guard. Before a car could enter the secure area, it was searched, and a mirror on a long pole was run under the vehicle.

It didn't take rocket science to conclude that this was not the area in which to confront Pedro Martinelli. As Grant was turning to leave, he caught a glimpse of a man in a white suit leaving a side door of the palace, followed by two of the ubiquitous young men in dark suits and sunglasses. Grant crossed the street and joined a tour group that was listening to their guide. As the men passed, he noticed the platform boots and scarred face, which gave Martinelli a cruel look. His missing ear was hidden by long, wavy black hair.

Grant gave them a block's head start, crossed the street, and began following them.

Ten minutes later, Martinelli went into a beautifully restored art deco building situated on a corner with circular overhanging wrought iron bal-conies on the second and third floors. The suits peeled off and headed back toward the palace. Grant put the map in front of his face as they passed him and then slipped into a doorway to observe the building.

A short time later, a woman in a black dress with a white apron came out onto the third-floor balcony and began watering plants. A moment later, Martinelli came out, lit a cigarette, and ran his hand up the woman's dress.

"Gotcha," said Grant to himself.

CHAPTER 30

El Chapo sat alone on the deck of the Cabo villa, nursing a cup of coffee as the eastern sky lightened. Emma, his wife, had returned unexpectedly from Los Angeles with their newborn daughter. Her arrival meant he'd had to banish his other women to a nearby villa. She put up with his womanizing but would not tolerate having her face rubbed in it.

The baby girl was cute but didn't stir any feelings in him. His son from an earlier marriage had been killed by a Sanchez family assassin several years ago and, although he wouldn't admit it, the pain lingered. He'd told Emma he didn't want any children, but she'd allowed it to happen, claiming it had been an accident. He'd told her to get an abortion, but she'd refused, claiming to be a good Catholic. Bullshit. She was a good Catholic only when it served her purposes. He had his needs, which she hadn't serviced while pregnant, and now, as a new mother, she wasn't getting with the program. He needed her to get back in shape; there were plenty of nannies to be had. This mother bit was pissing him off. He'd give her a little more time to get used to being a mother, but then she was going to have to get her priorities straight. If not...well, she wasn't going to have a choice—that was not how it worked with him.

The brighter side of her return was fewer distractions from dealing with his current problems.

Hector Sanchez was forming a new national police force, ten thousand strong, allegedly to fight the drug cartels. The only cartel Sanchez intended to fight was the Sinaloa cartel. El Chapo knew where this new special police force was coming from—the Zetas. Sanchez was putting those animals in police uniforms, giving them the imprimatur of the government, and sending them to Sinaloa to bring him to heel. He couldn't bribe the Zetas, and he didn't trust them to live up to the terms of any alliance they might form. It might cost less in lives and money to resume payments to the Sanchez family.

What worried him the most was Hector Sanchez trying to restore the pyramid shape of the drug business, with the Zetas just below the government and the other cartels below the Zetas.

Vicente Fox, the former president of Mexico, had made a mess of things by toppling the old pyramid and creating a horizontal structure, which was no structure at all. It had caused the deaths of over one hundred thousand people during his so-called war on the cartels.

El Chapo had a different vision: a parallel universe where the government and the cartels left one another alone. He didn't think that could happen while Hector Sanchez was president of Mexico. Maybe he should explore a treaty with Sanchez and resume the payoffs until he left office. Put enough money behind a candidate who he could control. Maybe even turn the government against the Sanchez family.

El Chapo lit a fine Honduran cigar and sat in a cloud of smoke as he turned his attention to Grant Meredith. The men he sent to Bocas Town to deal with Meredith said he had disappeared. He still had a room, which held his and Chambers's clothes, but he was not there. He needed to get rid of Meredith and Chambers so he could deal with his more pressing problems. He took his time enjoying his cigar and thinking.

The only plan he could come up with was way too obvious—they would make a ransom demand for the return of the Chambers woman, maybe a million dollars to be delivered somewhere in Bocas by Meredith alone. Then they would simply take the money and kill him and the woman. Straightforward, simple, and hard to fuck up. The best plans were always simple.

CHAPTER 31

Grant had been drinking coffee at a café across from Martinelli's building for almost two hours when he emerged at ten that evening, trailing two bodyguards. A few blocks later, they turned into the twelve-room Tantalo Hotel and disappeared into the elevator. A good guess was that they were heading to the rooftop bar.

As Grant emerged from the elevator, he was engulfed in a fog of humidity reeking of perfume, sweat, alcohol, and cheap cologne. A few strings of lights barely illuminated a throng of sweating twentysomethings yelling to be heard over the throbbing music. Without the spectacular view of Casco Viejo, it could have been a club in Vegas. As Grant was surveying the roof for Martinelli, an intoxicated woman in shorts and a halter top bounced off him, leaving a smear of sweat on his shirt.

Grant saw Martinelli across the roof and moved to the edge of the crowd to avoid any more of the writhing dancers. As he watched, Martinelli's bodyguards encouraged a couple to move from one of the few tall round-topped tables scattered along the parapet of the roof. Martinelli sat, and one of his bodyguards went to the bar and got him a drink while the other approached an attractive dark-haired woman and, after a brief conversation, pointed to Martinelli. She looked over, shook her head no, and returned to her companions. Unperturbed, the bodyguard moved to a short, dark-haired, slightly overweight woman, who accepted the invitation to join Martinelli at his recently acquired table. This type of solicitation reminded Grant of the allegations that state troopers had solicited women for a former governor who had become president.

The woman settled onto the empty stool strategically placed to Martinelli's right with the high table between them and the dancers. One of the bodyguards got her a drink. Two drinks later, she giggled when Martinelli nuzzled her neck and nipped her ear. His next move was a hand to her knee, which she deliberately removed. A few minutes later, he put his hand back, and when she did not immediately remove it, he slipped his hand up her thigh toward the short hem of her dress. Grant watched in amusement as she pivoted off the stool and landed a vicious slap on Martinelli's cheek. Before he could react, she disappeared into the crowd. Martinelli rubbed his cheek, motioned for his bodyguards, and left.

Grant followed the trio back to Martinelli's apartment and saw him dismiss the bodyguards at the front door. A minute later the lights on the third floor came on.

Grant stood in the doorway of the closed café across the street from the apartment building and checked his watch—two in the morning. All the surrounding buildings were dark, but faint reggae music was floating on the light breeze, and a few revelers heading home from the bars were still on the street. He wasn't going to get a better opportunity to get Martinelli alone. Now he needed to get into the building.

Trying to keep things simple, Grant crossed the cobblestone street and tried the front door. Unsurprisingly, it was locked. He started around the block and found that the building adjacent to Martinelli's was being renovated. He looked up and down the street—no pedestrians. The front of the building was covered by netting to protect passersby from falling debris. Grant pulled the netting away from the side of the building and stepped inside. His stood still and listened as his eyes adjusted to the darkness. The silence was punctuated by the unmistakable sound of someone snoring. Grant pulled out his mobile phone and enabled the flashlight app, which lit up the floor enough for him to see where he was going. Five steps into the building, he saw a lump against the wall, which was the source of the snoring—probably a homeless person. Grant slipped silently past him and up the stairs to the roof.

Once on the roof, all he had to do was step over the parapet onto the roof of Martinelli's building. He crossed the roof and looked over the edge. Directly below him was Martinelli's balcony, which was illuminated by interior lights. Grant hung from the roof and dropped silently onto the balcony. A French door into the living room was open, and Grant slipped inside.

Off to the left was an opening into a lighted room. Grant moved silently to the side of the door and pressed his back against the wall. From this position he could hear a shower running. He moved into the bedroom, positioned himself outside the bathroom door, and waited for Martinelli.

A few minutes later, Martinelli emerged, naked and drying his hair with a towel. Grant stepped behind him and caught his throat in the crook of his arm, applying pressure to the carotid artery and cutting off blood flow to Martinelli's brain. After a brief struggle, he collapsed in Grant's arms. Grant lowered him to the floor and went in search of a straight-backed chair, which he found in the breakfast room of the apartment. He pulled the cord off the bedroom blinds and tied Martinelli securely to the chair.

Unconscious, naked, and tied to a chair, Martinelli looked vulnerable, but Grant had no idea how he would react when he awoke. There wasn't going to be enough time to wear him down mentally—a trained operative could probably hold out for the two or so hours left before dawn. He had no idea if Martinelli had any training or how tough he was. Grant paced the room for a while and made his decision.

He went to the kitchen and pulled out two big pots. One he filled with ice and water, and the other he filled with water and put on the stove to boil. He picked up a butcher knife, a washrag, and a role of duct tape he found in a drawer.

Back in the bedroom, Martinelli was beginning to stir. Grant pulled his head back, stuffed the washrag in his mouth, and secured it with duct tape. Then he taped Martinelli's eyes shut. Satisfied with his work, Grant picked up the pot of ice water and poured it on Martinelli's head.

Grant watched as Martinelli's head jerked up and he tried to move. Realizing he was tied and couldn't see, Martinelli frantically pulled against the cords that secured him to the chair. He jerked so violently that the chair tipped over and his head hit the floor with a thud.

Grant silently righted the chair and whispered in his ear. "Fighting won't do you any good. You belong to me and will answer my questions. If you don't, you will suffer greatly."

Grant went to the kitchen and returned with a small pan of boiling water, which he held inches from Martinelli's face. Martinelli thrust his head backward, away from the boiling water.

Grant moved behind him and again whispered in his ear. "I'm going to ask you some questions, and you will answer by nodding your head up and down for yes and moving it sideways for no. If you fail to answer or give me a false answer, I'm going to pour this water over your head. Do you understand?"

Martinelli moved his head up and down in a tentative motion.

"Were you in Bocas del Toro three days ago?" Grant asked.

Martinelli's body stiffened, and Grant watched the tensed muscles.

"From now on, I will only ask a question once; if you do not answer immediately, I will dump this water on your head. Were you in Bocas del Toro three days ago?"

Martinelli nodded. This was a good start.

"Did you take a woman from the Nine Degrees restaurant?"

Martinelli hesitated, and Grant poured the scalding water on his head. Martinelli's scream was muffled by the duct tape, and he thrashed so hard that he tipped the chair over again. For the second time, his head hit the floor with an audible thump.

Grant righted the chair and watched as Martinelli frantically tried to inhale enough air through his nose. In pain from the burns on his scalp, cheeks, and neck, Martinelli was beginning to panic from lack of oxygen.

Grant calmly whispered in his ear, "I'm going to take the tape off your mouth. If you make even one sound, I will cut your throat and watch you bleed out. Do you understand?"

Martinelli frantically bobbed his head up and down.

Grant jerked the tape off Martinelli's mouth and pulled out the wash-rag. Martinelli gasped for air.

Just before Martinelli's breathing normalized, Grant slapped him across his burned cheek. "I have a plastic bag here that will fit nicely over your head. Answer my questions or that is how you die."

Martinelli nodded slowly.

"Where did you take the woman from Nine Degrees?"

Martinelli inhaled slowly and quietly said, "I don't know what happened to her. The Mexicans took her."

"Where?"

"I swear on my mother's grave, I don't know."

This seemed a little too easy, but then Martinelli was weak. An asshole with women and a coward with men; he would rather spill his guts than suffer any further pain.

"Why did you take her?"

Again Martinelli hesitated. Grant picked up the butcher knife and made a superficial cut on Martinelli's forearm, which jerked reflexively. Grant pulled Martinelli's good ear away from his head and placed the knife firmly against his skull, with the blade touching the top of the ear.

"I have no more patience for you. Answer the question or I am going to cut off this ear and shove it down your throat."

"You're going to get me killed," Martinelli said.

Grant put enough pressure on the knife blade to draw blood, which trickled down the side of Martinelli's neck.

"Okay, okay. Guzman—El Chapo—told me to do it. The woman and some guy had been nosing around Red Frog Beach. El Chapo thought she and this guy might be working for the DEA or maybe the Sanchez family. After I spoke to her, I told El Chapo she was just a tourist, but he wasn't so sure. The Mexicans dropped me off and left with her. I don't know what happened to her…honest. Please don't hurt me anymore."

Grant removed the knife and looked at his watch—five in the morning. The sky was filled with gray dawn. Not much time left.

"Where do I find El Chapo?" asked Grant.

"Mexico. He moves around. I don't know."

The sound of an electric buzzer broke the silence.

Still whispering, Grant asked, "What is that?"

"The intercom from downstairs. My security men are here," said Martinelli tentatively, not sure what reaction that was going to engender in his captor.

No more time. The bodyguards had a job to do, and they wouldn't wait downstairs very long if Martinelli did not buzz them in. Martinelli probably had a lot more details, but he wasn't the main guy—it was El Chapo. Shit, how could Stephanie be in worse trouble?

Grant put a strip of duct tape across Martinelli's mouth and loosened the cords that secured him to the chair. "If anything happens to that woman, I will be back to slowly peel off your skin and cut you into little pieces. For your own sake, you had better persuade El Chapo to let her go unharmed."

Grant swiftly left the bedroom and headed for the balcony. There he climbed on top of a table and jumped, grabbing the parapet and pulling himself back up on the roof. One minute later he exited the building next door and walked away from Martinelli's building.

CHAPTER 32

Grant returned to Canal House and took a long, hot shower before heading to the library on the first floor. Plush furniture, bookcases, and a Zapotec rug made the small room a quiet retreat from the street noise outside. Grant brewed a cup of coffee in the K-cup machine and settled into a wingback chair by the window. The smell of coffee and the flowers on the sideboard were filtered through the concrete dust that lingered in his nostrils from the construction site next to Martinelli's building. His interrogation of Martinelli had been a bust. Stephanie had been gone three days, and he was no closer to finding her.

He had not heard anything from Scammon or Turnbull, so there had not been a ransom demand left at his hotel in Bocas Town. El Chapo was in Mexico. Neither the Mexican nor the US government could find him, so it was not likely that Grant would fare any better.

He could kidnap Martinelli and hold him for an exchange, but that would create an international incident. And anyway, to a man like El Chapo, Martinelli was disposable.

Grant began to pace the room. He glanced at the local newspaper on the sideboard and recognized one of the men in the picture on the front page above the fold—Hector Sanchez. His limited Spanish allowed him to decipher that Hector was in Panama City for an inter-Americas conference being held at the Trump Ocean Club hotel.

Stephanie had been Hector's mistress for a short while before she had helped Grant escape from the Sanchez family. That episode had surely embarrassed Hector. She had also threated Hector and the entire Sanchez family when Carlos had been hell-bent on killing Grant. But all of that didn't necessarily mean he wouldn't help. In theory, El Chapo worked for the Sanchez family. Maybe Hector would be willing to put some pressure on him to release Stephanie? Grant made another cup of coffee and thought about how to get in touch with Hector. One didn't just knock on the door of his hotel room.

He had never asked Stephanie about her time with Hector. He had thought about it a lot, particularly after their time in Bora Bora, but had finally decided he didn't really want to know if she still had feelings for Hector. She had helped him escape, but that didn't mean whatever feelings she may have had for the man had ended. It was complicated. He didn't understand what she had been doing with Hector in the first place. If Hector helped rescue her, would she go back to him?

Grant tried the simplest way first and called the hotel, asking for Hector. The operator said Hector did not take direct calls and connected him with Hector's assistant, where he got a message machine. Grant left a message.

"This is Grant Meredith. Please have President Sanchez call me as soon as possible regarding Stephanie Chambers." He left his cell number and hung up.

Then Grant called Bob Edgar at the Trump Ocean Club. When he said he was calling about a security issue, he was transferred to Edgar's cell phone.

"Edgar."

"This is Grant Meredith. I need some help."

"Look, I've got the presidents of ten Latin American countries in this hotel. I don't have time to shit, much less help you. Maybe next week."

"It won't take any time. I just need you to give a note to Hector Sanchez."

"Christ, Meredith, do it yourself."

"You're running security there. You know I won't be able to get into the hotel, much less get close enough to talk to him or pass a note."

Edgar paused. "What's this note going to say?"

"He's an old friend of Stephanie's; I'm going to ask him to help me find her."

"All right, I'll meet you in the lobby at ten, but I'm going to read the note first."

The seventy-story Trump Ocean Club Hotel and Tower was jammed among other high-rises on the Punta Pacifica peninsula fronting the Bay of Panama. The high-ceilinged, hard-surfaced marble-and-granite lobby seemed sterile and cold to Grant when he arrived promptly at ten. Edgar read the note and promised to get it to President Sanchez.

CHAPTER 33

Hector Sanchez stood on the balcony of his suite at the Trump Ocean Club while he read the note from Grant Meredith. He was stunned. Stephanie Chambers was the only woman who had ever run away from him. Women didn't do that. He tired of them at some point and sent them away with generous deposits in their bank accounts. He hadn't tired of Stephanie; in fact, he had been depressed at her loss until he'd hooked up with Bianca Flores, a lithe eighteen-year-old beauty queen from Veracruz. Now *there* was a sexual athlete.

Stephanie. They had connected sexually, but it had been more than that for him. He'd wanted her to want him, really want to be with him, but he had always felt that she was just along for the ride. Most of the women he bedded were in it for the thrill of sleeping with the president of Mexico, the high life, and the excitement of private jets, splashy parties, and ocean-front villas. They came to him with the emotional maturity of teenagers.

Stephanie had always been different. He, of course, knew she had been an assassin for the CIA, but nevertheless, she was a lady. He had never treated her like the other disposable women who passed through his life. Everything about her was different; in the final analysis, he respected her as a woman, an equal. He had put her out of his mind, but now that she was back in it, he missed her.

Grant Meredith had stood up to his father, Carlos—something few men did and lived. Hector didn't think of him as having taken Stephanie away from him. Stephanie had saved Meredith from being killed by Carlos. It was one time she hadn't looked the other way in family matters.

The situation had done something to her, like putting her back on track. Stephanie helping Meredith to escape didn't make Hector angry. Meredith meant nothing to him; he had been Carlos's obsession. He would meet with Meredith and find out what he wanted. If Stephanie needed help, he would consider it.

CHAPTER 34

Grant had just returned to La Casona when his cell phone rang. The man on the other end identified himself as an aide to President Sanchez. He instructed Grant to be in the hotel lobby promptly at five thirty that evening, where he would be met and escorted to meet the president. He curtly warned Grant that he would only have ten minutes for the meeting.

Two burly men in dark suits with earpieces were waiting for Grant as he entered the lobby. They led him to the bell captain's storage room off the lobby and professionally searched him from head to toe. His pockets were emptied onto a table, and the contents were placed in a lead-lined box, which they handed to a hotel security officer on the way out.

The men escorted Grant to a suite on the thirty-fifth floor and knocked. The door was opened by another man, slimmer than the others, with the obligatory earpiece. He stepped aside and ushered Grant into an elegantly sterile room with a cold white-and-beige décor. Floor-to-ceiling windows opened onto a huge balcony overlooking the Bay of Panama.

Hector, dressed in a white tropical suit and an open-collared royal-blue shirt, rose from the desk, where he had been reading some papers, and, without a word, gestured Grant to take a seat on what proved to be an uncomfortable snow-white sofa. Hector took a chair facing Grant and carefully arranged the crease in his trousers. He took his time picking a cigar from a box on the table, carefully snipping off the end with a gold cigar cutter, and lighting it with a gold Dunhill lighter. He did not offer one to Grant. After drawing on his cigar and studying the lighted end, he finally turned to Grant and addressed him in cultured, unaccented English.

"Part of me wants to have you thrown off the balcony to feed the fish. Yes, a rather large part of me wants to do that. However, I do have fond memories of Ms. Chambers, despite her hasty departure from my hospitality."

As Hector casually looked at his watch, Grant noted his movie-star good looks and aura of elegance that reminded him of a Latin Cary Grant.

"I don't have much time, so tell me all you know about her disappearance."

Grant told him everything that had happened, glossing over his trouble with the local police and buying weapons.

Hector silently smoked as he considered Grant's information. Then, looking at the tip of his cigar, he said casually, "Guzman again. The man is a thorn in my side, or, as you Americans say somewhat inelegantly, a pain in my ass. It is interesting that the Sinaloa cartel is smuggling drugs through Bocas del Toro…very interesting. But I'm not sure I can be of any help locating Stephanie in Panama. Why should I care what happens to her?"

Grant inhaled slowly as he sat back in his chair and willed himself to relax. "Mr. President, with respect, if you didn't care, you would not have agreed to this meeting."

The ghost of a smile appeared on Hector's face and quickly vanished. "Perhaps, but even if I could help, what's the point—she will just return to the United States with you."

"Stephanie can and will do what she wants. However, if you help rescue her, it would be a humanitarian triumph and wonderful publicity. Additionally, there's a political point. I read that you're sending troops after the Sinaloa cartel. Rescuing Stephanie from Guzman would be a blow against him and would show that you are in control, not him."

Hector smoked his cigar silently while he studied Grant. His aide entered the room and stood, waiting. Hector looked at his watch and stood. Grant stood also.

"After receiving your note, I spoke to President Martinelli about Ms. Chambers's disappearance. With regrets, he was unable to offer assistance.

I don't believe him, but there you are. At the end of our conversation, he mentioned that any BlackRock contractors found in Panama would be treated as enemies of the state. However, I can tell you that we are getting close to Guzman; your DEA has been assisting with valuable intelligence. When he is captured, I will discuss Ms. Chambers with him. I wish you well in your search. Now, you will have to excuse me."

———

Grant knew it had been a long shot. Hector had probably meant well in contacting President Martinelli, but it had backfired. Obviously, the president was working with the cartel. His threat concerning BlackRock operators took them off the table. At least Grant now knew the situation and would not risk their capture.

CHAPTER 35

The Zetas' execution of ten Culiacán police on the Sinaloa payroll, whose heads had been impaled on the wrought-iron fence surrounding the police station, brought El Chapo back to his ranch in the Sinaloa mountains. From there he intended to direct the defense of Culiacán, the largest city and capital of Sinaloa and key to the cartel's operations.

He had no sooner arrived than he got a call from Pedro Martinelli, telling him in great detail how he had been tortured and threatened by an unknown assailant who demanded the release of Chambers. Martinelli assured him that he had told the assailant nothing. El Chapo believed him because Martinelli didn't know what had happened to her.

"Calm down, you did well. It had to have been Meredith who attacked you. He's the only one we know of who would do something like that. If it wasn't him, it was one of his BlackRock bastards. You have the picture of him I sent you earlier, so you know what he looks like," said El Chapo.

Martinelli exploded. "That son of a bitch poured boiling water on my head. I'm going to have him picked up for questioning."

"Listen to me very carefully. I have plans for him and Chambers. If you pick him up, he goes into the system, and the Americans may get involved. Leave him alone for now. Do you understand me?"

"Make him suffer."

El Chapo hung up.

Next came the news that the night before, Zetas crashed a birthday party for the mayor of Culiacán and opened fire on the tables where Sinaloa cartel members were sitting. His men were armed, and a firefight erupted. Three of his men died before Sinaloa reinforcements arrived and caught the Zetas in a cross fire. All seven Zetas were killed. The mayor had been saved by a stroke of luck. Brazil's Miss BumBum 2014 had been sitting on his lap and took a stray round in her ample hip, which would otherwise have hit the mayor.

El Chapo needed to focus on the Zetas and whether to make peace with the Sanchez family before Sinaloa drowned in blood. Meredith and Chambers were distractions that he didn't have any more time to fool with.

He called Mr. Bond on a disposable cell phone, which would be discarded after this call.

"Where are you with the Chambers woman?" asked El Chapo.

"Just getting started. These things take time, but she'll break eventually," said Bond.

"No time. Change of plans. She's working for the DEA or Sanchez or she was in the wrong place at the wrong time—I no longer care. I want to use her as bait to get to Meredith and then kill them both. Have your men ready to move her to Beverly's Hill, that little rooming house in Old Bank, when I give the word. Meredith will be coming to ransom her, and we will kill them both."

"All right. Do you want me to work on her between now and then?"

"Do you think you can get anything useful out of her in a couple days?"

"Probably not."

"Then why bother?"

"You never know what might happen."

El Chapo sighed. He hated sadists. For them, inflicting pain was an end in itself.

"That's my point exactly—you don't know what might happen. You get too enthusiastic and she dies. What I want you to do is get me a picture to prove she's alive. Take today's newspaper out there and take a picture of her with it."

"I'll do it, but with today's technology, Meredith could figure we photoshopped the picture," said Bond.

"Maybe, but I'll tell him it will be a simultaneous exchange, so if he doesn't see her, he can back off."

"I don't know. That guy is pretty smart. He'll smell a trap," said Bond.

"He wants that woman back real bad; he'll do what he's told to do. Just like you. Now get me the picture," said El Chapo, hanging up without waiting for a reply.

———

The quiet noise of an idling outboard motor jolted Stephanie from a deep, dreamless sleep—the first restful sleep she had gotten in three days. Turning the peanut butter cap into two sharp-edged weapons had dispelled her feeling of helplessness and allowed her to sleep for too long. Bond and his two MS-13 gangsters were already on the walkway. She stood up quickly, but by then they were at her door. The makeshift knives were across the room on the kitchen counter.

Bond was at the door, carrying a newspaper. "I have good news for you, Ms. Chambers. My employer is going to offer you for ransom. We need to provide proof of life. Move the chair to the far side of the room and sit down."

Stephanie hesitated but had no chance to get to her weapons. Maybe she wouldn't need them now, but what if Bond saw them?

"Do it now," growled Bond, losing some of his Australian accent in the process.

Stephanie moved the chair and sat.

Bond unlocked the door, and the three men came in and stopped ten feet from her. Bond slid the newspaper across the floor. One of the MS-13 goons licked his lips lasciviously, while the other stared at her chest.

"Pick it up and hold it in front of you," said Bond in his restored Australian accent.

Stephanie did as she was told, and Bond used his phone to take a picture. He tapped the touch screen, apparently sending the picture to someone.

"I see you fixed your finger." Bond smiled. "Most regrettable, but then I suppose you learned a lesson."

Stephanie inhaled and exhaled slowly and then nodded. There was no point in risking another broken finger. She needed to get the men out of there before one of them saw her weapons.

"Good girl. You are a quick learner."

Bond's phone chirped. He looked at it and muttered, "Done."

The men left, and Stephanie slumped in the chair. Thank God they hadn't seen her weapons.

CHAPTER 36

Grant was in The Canal House's library using his Blackberry to catch up on e-mails that were in his BlackRock inbox. It was a public account in the sense that anyone accessing the BlackRock website could send him an e-mail. He usually got junk and insulting politically oriented e-mails, which he deleted without reading. For reasons that escaped him, a public relations expert had convinced the board that this sort of access would soften the company's image. Grant didn't agree, but he went along with it. The only time he checked the account was when he had nothing else to do…like now.

There was a beep, and a new e-mail with the heading "Stephanie Chambers for sale" appeared at the top of the list. Grant opened the e-mail.

"You may have your woman for $1 million US cash. She will be available for pick up the day after tomorrow, Thursday, at Beverly's Hill in Old Bank, Bastimentos, at noon. At five minutes after noon, we will begin to peel off her skin very slowly. You will come alone and bring the cash. Proof of life attached."

Grant opened the attachment and studied Stephanie's picture. She looked all right except for the splint on her right little finger.

He sat back in his chair and sighed with relief—she was alive. The relief was short-lived. *Maybe* she was alive. They could have photoshopped the picture. She could already be dead, but he couldn't take any chances. It could be a trap with her as bait. It made sense that the kidnappers would want to keep the bait alive until they got the money. He was going to have to rely on that. Money wasn't the issue—he could have his investment manager at Goldman wire the funds to the Bank of Panama.

The issue was going alone. Bastimentos was an island, most of which was impenetrable jungle. There was no road to the island; sea or air was the only way. If one came in from the sea, there were clear sight lines from shore. While Delilah had said there was a path from Red Frog Beach, all the kidnappers needed to do was block the path with a couple men. Maybe BlackRock could drop a couple ex-Seals a few miles from shore and they could slip in. But once the town woke up in the morning, there would be no place to hide; in any event, he couldn't risk their capture by the Panamanian government.

Backup wasn't feasible—too much chance of an international incident. Shit.

Grant called New York and arranged for the wire transfer. Then he made arrangements for a charter aircraft to take him to Bocas Town. When he freed Stephanie, he wanted to get away as soon as possible and out of this damnable country.

CHAPTER 37

Stephanie used the jar cap to cut strips out of a small washcloth and carefully wrapped the cloth around the metal to create a handle of sorts for both parts of the cap. When she was done, there was a little over two inches of blade on each piece. Even if Grant paid a ransom, she didn't believe for a second that the men would let her go. She had seen too many faces. Before they killed her, Bond would have his fun trying to destroy any iota of self-respect she might have for herself in exchange for the false promise that he would let her live if she told him what he wanted to know. One of the lessons her father had drummed into her as a preteen was that self-respect couldn't be taken from you without your consent. She wasn't going to consent. She was going to fight, and she was going to win or die trying. That was her advantage—she was willing to die.

Next, she used one of the sharp edges to cut two strips off the bottom of her T-shirt. They would come in handy if she disabled someone and wanted to strangle them. Weapons ready, she sat down to plan how to attack the three men. After a while she decided on a plan but then remembered another thing her father had taught her. The first casualty of battle was usually the battle plan. She needed her plan, but she also needed to think about what could go wrong and how to react. It always came down to preparation.

The same three men would probably come for her. They would probably use the same approach: order her to sit in the chair with her back to them while they came through the door and crossed the room to tie her to the chair. Last time all three had stayed behind her until she was tied, but only one of them had tied her to the chair. She needed them in the room and close to her.

She had no recollection of any of them carrying side arms. The goons were only wearing shorts with no place to hide a pistol. Theoretically, they could have carried small knives in their pockets, but she didn't think they did. Bond's polo shirt had been tucked into his jeans. She remembered no bulges indicating a pistol under his shirt. They weren't armed. Three of them against a woman—they weren't worried about her. They were men; they were in control; they were overconfident. She had offered no resistance, so there was no reason for them to change their method of operating. Their actions would be predictable. That would be her second advantage.

Stephanie mentally rehearsed her moves. Finally, she assumed the lotus position and meditated.

CHAPTER 38

The faint sound of an outboard motor broke the stillness that preceded full dark. They were coming. Stephanie tried to swallow but couldn't. She took a drink from her water bottle, held the liquid in her mouth, swished it around, and spit it in the sink. Dampness under her arms in the absence of exercise was an unfamiliar sensation. Her heart rate was increasing. Tightness in her chest made it difficult to breathe. A solitary drop of sweat made its descent along her spine. As the panga nosed through the overgrown channel from the sea, she wiped damp palms on her pants. She had killed people before, but it had been from a distance, with a rifle. This was going to be up close, very personal, and very bloody. She took a deep breath, exhaled slowly, and rolled her shoulders. It wouldn't be long now.

Stephanie moved to the side of her cage to watch. There were only two men in the panga—a sign of good fortune? She remembered the nervous feeling before innumerable track-and-field competitions. There were also nervous moments before an assassination. What both activities had in common was once the event was underway, there were no nerves, only execution, which she had trained for over and over. She was trained and she was ready for life's ultimate challenge—kill or be killed.

She inhaled deeply and exhaled, slowing her heart rate.

She placed the chair where she wanted it, with the back to the door.

She picked up her blades, one in each hand. She turned the sharp ends upward along the inside of her wrists, keeping her broken little finger out of the way.

She watched the panga approach.

It was the MS-13 goons; no Bond. Once again they were clad only in shorts and sandals. Bulging muscles were covered in tattoos. Snakes wound up their legs, with the heads disappearing under their shorts. One's chest was covered with a dragon blowing fire. The other's chest had a large skull with snakes crawling out of its eye sockets. Stephanie stopped focusing on the tattooed torsos and looked for weapons. As before, she saw none.

As they approached the door, they were preceded by the smell of testosterone-fueled sweat and something else...something like day-old chicken left in the garbage pail. Stephanie focused on their eyes: yellowed and shot through with broken blood vessels, peering from within tattooed faces—hideous Halloween masks.

Something in their eyes was a little off. They were dull, with no sign of alertness or anticipation. Drugs...they had taken something.

Stephanie had read about Mexican sicarios getting high on cocaine before mutilating people who were still alive and cutting up their bodies. Had these two snorted enough to impair their judgment and, hopefully, their motor skills?

Cholo leered at her through the door and gestured toward the chair with a length of rope. A memory of him pulling down his shorts flashed before her eyes.

Stephanie sat with her feet firmly placed on the floor. Her hands rested lightly on her thighs, palms down. All her senses were on edge.

There was the metal-on-metal scraping sound as the door was opened.

Four bare feet padded across the floor toward her.

The sound stopped.

She sensed one of them directly behind her and the other goon beside him on the left. She turned her head ever so slightly and, from the corner of her eye, confirmed their positions.

A mist of rotten chicken engulfed her as the man behind her lowered his head and reached for her left arm. As he began to pull her arm behind her, she slid the piece of sharpened metal in her right hand from behind her wrist and drove it back as hard as she could into the inside of his right thigh. When the bottom of her palm reached flesh, she simultaneously stood and pulled upward, using the leverage of her legs to rip the sharpened metal through his femoral artery. In a continuous motion, she whirled to her left, shifting the blade in her right hand, and lunged into the other goon, driving the sharpened metal into his neck. She jerked the blade violently upward, severing his carotid artery.

Cholo lay on the floor, his severed artery pumping blood, which pooled around him. The other man's carotid artery spewed blood everywhere as he turned, trying to stop the spray with his hands. Stephanie stood, covered in blood, in an expanding pool of the red, sticky liquid.

Her attack had taken less than two seconds. Three minutes later, both men had bled out and were dead.

She quickly searched their pockets—empty.

Stephanie took a quick shower and let the water rinse away the blood. She rinsed out her clothes and put them on wet.

She had executed her plan flawlessly, but she had been lucky there were only two of them. She had been lucky they were high, dulling their reflexes, and she had been exceptionally lucky Bond hadn't been there. The third man would have had time to react, to defend himself or attack her.

So much for the after-action analysis. It was always better to be lucky than good; fortunately, she had been both. As she moved toward the door, she kicked something, which rolled across the floor to the door—Cholo's glass eye

The panga's motor started easily, and she pulled away from the dock toward the opening in the mangroves. The movement of the panga stirred her hair. She shook her head and took pleasure in the breeze. The salty smell of sea air filled her nostrils, replacing the iron smell of blood. Out there was the sea...freedom.

CHAPTER 39

Stephanie nosed the panga through the mangroves and into the sea. Then it hit her—she didn't know where she was. She couldn't make out any landmasses around her. Was the land behind her part of the mainland or an island? What country was she in? Stephanie remembered another of her father's lessons: the bigger the crisis, the more you have to calm down and think. There was no room for panic, only rational thought. He'd had exactly zero tolerance for teenage faux crises. He had been patient about it but had made her think her way out of each one.

It was highly likely she was still in Central American, given the vegetation. Most probably Panama, since the men had taken her in a panga, which was not exactly an ocean-going vessel. The farther they took her, the more risk they ran; that supported Panama. Unfortunately, she must be some distance from Bocas Town, since there was no light on the horizon. But then again, Bocas Town was not exactly Disneyland. She would assume Panama, Isla Colon or Bastimentos probably; other islands in the archipelago were farther away.

There was no fuel can in the panga, so her captors had come from a place where they could get to her and back on one tank of gas. That was a good sign but also a problem. If she took off in the wrong direction, she could run out of gas in the middle of nowhere.

She ran the panga straight out from the shoreline about a quarter mile, idled the engine, turned to face the shore, and looked around again. Still the only landmass in sight was in front of her; still no artificial light on the horizon. She was going to have to go somewhere, so she should at least know in which direction she was going to travel. As a child, she and her father had lain in the grass, looking at the night sky while he taught her celestial navigation. Although the general principles had stuck with her, she had always thought it interesting but useless information. Now it might save her life.

Bocas del Toro was nine degrees north of the equator. The key to celestial navigation in the Northern Hemisphere was the North Star. Stephanie searched the night sky and found the Big Dipper, the two pointer stars, and finally the North Star. It was behind her, directly opposite the landmass. That was good. Panama ran east to west, not north to south as one might think. So right was west and left was east. Her direction of travel was known, but not her destination. Either choice gave her at least a fifty-fifty chance. She would follow the shoreline west.

After an hour, nothing had changed except she had used an hour's worth of gas and was thirsty. It was still dark. She could continue on, turn around, or sit and wait for daylight to make a more informed decision. She decided to cut the engine and drift until there was some light. With luck there might be a house right in front of her that she couldn't see in the darkness.

In the gray first light of dawn, she saw nothing but jungle on the land in front of her. Her thirst was becoming a problem. She could pull onto the shore and look for water, but there was no guarantee she would find any, and there were poisonous snakes. She wasn't that desperate yet.

Stephanie continued westward. A half hour later, the sun was up, reflecting off the ocean and scorching the back of her neck and her back through her T-shirt. Her lips had dried out completely, and she had no moisture in her mouth.

Then, almost without realizing it, she ran past the landmass into the open ocean. She checked her fuel—not much left. That meant she should have gone east. There wasn't enough fuel to get back to her starting point, and even if she could and then travel farther east, there was a reasonable chance that by now someone had come looking for the MS-13 goons and she would run into them. There really wasn't a choice; she would continue around the headland until she found something on the shoreline or ran out of gas. If that happened, she would have to trust her luck to the jungle.

As she rounded the headland, the reflected sun struck her full in the face. No hat, no sunglasses, and, of course, no sun block. Her face was frying. She still couldn't swallow. Something was going to have to happen soon.

CHAPTER 40

As the sun beat down on Stephanie, a Cessna Citation Mustang landed smoothly at the small Bocas Town Airport in the cool morning air. Grant hustled through the terminal and found Turnbull leaning against a '57 Chevy Bel Air, which was being eaten by rust. During the five-minute ride to Grant's hotel, he brought Turnbull up to date.

Turnbull pulled to the side of the road by the hotel and, as Grant moved to get out of the car, grabbed his arm. "Grant, you can't go there alone without backup. It's crazy. They'll just kill you and take the money."

Grant pulled his arm free. "I can't risk blowing the chance to get her back. I'll have my guns; I don't care about the money. Get Delilah and meet me in the bar here in ten minutes. There's something you can do to help."

Grant, Turnbull, and Delilah huddled at a waterside table in the empty bar. Their intensity contrasted with the boats drifting by under a cloudless blue sky and the gentle swell of the Caribbean lapping against the dock. Grant gave them a few minutes to make their case that he shouldn't go alone. They were convincing, but Grant was immovable. Finally, he held up his hand to cut them off.

"Please, I appreciate your concern, but I'm going to go alone. I'm going to rent a boat with a powerful motor because when I leave Old Bank, I'll be leaving at full speed. I need you to meet me at the dock when I…we come in. The pilot will be in the plane. When you see me coming, call him to start the engine. When we hit the dock, you drive me to the plane, and we're out of here. Can you do that for me?"

Turnbull and Delilah looked at one another and reluctantly nodded.

When Grant left to find a boat, Turnbull and Delilah looked at one another.

"We can't let him go alone, Delilah. I'm going to follow him in a water taxi."

"And do zactly what?" snapped Delilah.

Turnbull opened his mouth, but no sound came out. After a moment, he closed his mouth. "I don't know, but we have to do something. We can't let him get killed."

Delilah put her hands on his shoulders and fixed her eyes on his. "We ain't lettin' him git kilt. If'n he gets his head blowed off, it's his own damn fault. He's a fool, plain and simple. Thar ain't nuttin' yuh ken do fer fools. They's too ingenious."

Turnbull raised his arms violently and knocked her hands off his shoulders. He clenched his fists, and his face turned an angry red. "Goddamn it, Delilah, I'm going to do something. I've got to. I can't let him get himself killed. I won't."

Delilah took a step back and looked at Turnbull with her head slightly cocked. In the years she had known him, he had never cursed, much less cursed at her. Now she wasn't sure she knew him as well as she'd thought. The man she knew carried guilt that was rotting his soul. A drunk, yes, but there were a few sober moments when he was loveable—something more than a man willing to satisfy her sexual urges without any strings. But never this. He hadn't been the same since she'd sobered him up and he'd gone with Meredith to Red Frog Beach. She wanted to know this man, who now reminded her of the military men she had known and loved. Older by far, but there was grit there. She didn't agree but respected his desire to help Meredith.

Turnbull turned to leave, and she grabbed him by the arm. He shook her hand off and continued.

"Turnbull, stop...please. I kin help."

He hesitated and turned. "Why? There's no money in it for you."

Delilah hit him with a closed-fist roundhouse right that sent him staggering across the deck. She grabbed him before he fell.

"Becuz it's the right thing tuh do. Don yuh eva talk tuh me like that agin, got it?"

Turnbull, who was holding his jaw, nodded as she released him.

"I'm truly sorry, Delilah. My remark was totally uncalled for and no way for a gentleman to talk to a lady. Will you forgive me?"

Delilah, grinning, slowly shook her right hand and said, "Of course, yuh big oaf, but yer jaw nearly broke muh hand. Yuh surely got a hard head."

Turnbull grinned back and said, "Well, my head may be hard, but I think you knocked some sense into it. What have you got in mind?"

"Git that boat uh Samson's, the one wit the hard canopy, and meet me at the dock by the dive shop."

———

Thirty minutes later, Turnbull pulled up alongside the dock, and Delilah, carrying a long canvas duffel bag, dropped into the boat with a grace that defied her size.

"What's in the bag?"

"Git us out on the water an I'll show yuh."

During her marriage, Delilah had spent many of her idle hours on the JOTC firing range working with master firearms instructors. She had bested so many of the snipers who went through the program that it became a badge of honor within the sniper community to defeat her in a match.

When they were away from the dock, Delilah opened the duffel and pulled out a wicked-looking rifle. "This here's a CheyTac Intervention M200, a genuine 'merican-made sniper rifle."

Next, she held up a rifle cartridge. "This here's a .408-caliber copper-nickel-alloy cartridge that leaves the barrel at three thousand feet per second. Got itself a range uh twenty-five hunnert yards."

Delilah chambered a round and slapped in a seven-round magazine.

"Jesus, Delilah, where did you get that?"

"Won it back at JOTC when ole John was alive. He was surely durn proud uh me. Put three rounds within sixteen inches uh one 'nother at twenty-three hunnert yards. World record at the time. Pretty sweet if'n I do say so muhself."

Turnbull shook his head. "You are an amazing woman. That is a superb accomplishment, something to be very proud of. Why haven't you told me about this?"

"Fact is, yuh ain't been sober long enough to have such a conversation."

She gently put her hand on his forearm. "There's a lot more tuh me than my gorgeous body and sweet disposition."

Turnbull laughed and pointed the boat toward Bastimentos.

———

As Old Bank began to come into sight, Delilah told Turnbull to slow down.

"I'm needin yuh tuh pull up 'bout a quarter mile outta town so I kin get a line on Meredith and Beverly's Hill. Hittin' a target from farther out on an unstable platform liken this here boat be nigh on to impossible, particular since I ain't had any practice fur a coon's age."

CHAPTER 41

Stephanie had felt her skin frying for several hours before she saw an actual beach and what looked like a few houses or a settlement of some kind. She gunned the panga onto the beach and jumped ashore. Walking along the little beach toward her was a tall, thin black woman in a sarong with her hair wrapped in a colorful scarf. Stephanie broke into a stumbling run toward her.

When she reached the woman, she tried to speak but couldn't form words; there was no moisture in her mouth.

The woman held out a water bottle and said nothing while Stephanie rinsed her mouth, rubbed some water on her lips, and took a drink.

"Where am I?"

The woman looked closely at Stephanie, suspecting a joke of some kind, and answered with a Caribbean lilt in her voice. "Bocas del Drago, on the north side of Isla Colon, Panama."

"Oh, thank God," said Stephanie.

Now the woman's look turned skeptical. "Would you like to tell me what's going on?"

Stephanie took a deep breath and collected her thoughts, not sure how much she should share with this stranger.

She held out her hand. "Perhaps I should start by introducing myself. I'm Stephanie Chambers."

The woman took Stephanie's hand in both of hers. "I'm Astrid. They've been looking everywhere for you."

Stephanie was taken aback. "Who are *they* exactly?"

"My friend John Scammon has been helping a man named Meredith look for you. Where have you been?"

Stephanie ignored her question. "Do you have a cell phone I could borrow? I need to let Grant know I'm all right."

"Yes, of course, it's back at my house. Come, it's not far."

As they walked, Astrid said, "Girl, you are a mess. Where have you been?"

Stephanie walked along in silence, unsure who this woman was and what she knew about the events.

As the silence lingered, Astrid stepped right in front of Stephanie, well inside her personal space.

"Listen carefully, girl. Don't fuck with Astrid or I put the hex on you. If you want my help, I need some basic information. I live here. If you're in trouble, maybe it comes back to me, so open up."

Stephanie tried to step around her, but Astrid sidestepped in front of her and moved so close their bodies were almost touching. Stephanie considered shoving her out of the way but quickly realized what a bad idea that was. She needed help. She was so tired, it was easier to tell Astrid the truth—try to build a relationship and get some help.

They continued walking, and Stephanie told her about the kidnapping and being kept in a cage, glossing over how she escaped.

Without looking at her, Astrid nodded. "How many of them did you kill?"

Stephanie, stunned, stopped walking and turned to Astrid. "What... what are you talking about?"

"I'm talking about the blood under your fingernails and behind your left ear. There's also some dried blood in your left ear."

Stephanie reflexively looked at her nails and saw the crusted blood. "What makes you think that's blood?"

"Girl, I can smell it. Voodoo. I know many things, and one is the smell of blood."

Stephanie smelled her fingers. "I can't smell anything."

"That's because you don't have the gift. Don't worry, your secret is safe with me. Those goons deserved what they got."

CHAPTER 42

Grant had the seventy-five-horsepower outboard motor wide open as he sliced through the picture-perfect turquoise water on the way to Bastimentos. It was eleven forty-five in the morning; the sky was clear, and it was hot. The money was in a cotton duffel bag, with the Mossberg on top. The Glock was in his waistband, with an extra magazine in one of his cargo pockets. The other cargo pocket held shotgun shells. Ten minutes to the dock, and three minutes up to Beverly's Hill. He had no idea what would happen.

Grant pulled off Hellfly ballistic sunglasses and wiped the perspiration from his face with his T-shirt. The more he thought about it, the more he came to the obvious conclusion that this was a suicide mission. How could he be sure Stephanie would even be there? Why should the Mexicans let them go once they had the money? On the other hand, as long as there was some chance, he had to try. There hadn't been time to pull together a BlackRock team, and Turnbull would have just been in the way—something else to worry about. Hopefully they hadn't physically abused her, but there was no time to worry about that. If she was there, he was going to get her out. That's all there was to it.

Grant cut the engine and let the panga glide silently alongside the abandoned concrete pier. He stepped from the panga into a slight breeze that carried the smell of diesel fuel and human waste. As he surveyed the hillside above the pier, nothing moved; it was eerily quiet, as if the village had been abandoned.

There was a metallic taste in Grant's mouth as he slung the canvas bag over his left shoulder and moved across the pier with the Mossberg in his right hand. He pushed the safety switch off and left his finger along the stock outside the trigger guard, ready.

Grant spit as he moved up the crumbling steps, trying to get rid of the unwelcome taste. He reached the narrow concrete walkway that ran through Old Bank and slowly turned left toward the Beverly's Hill B and B; still no one in sight, nothing moving, no sound except the rapid beating of his heart. Grant stopped and took several deep breaths to slow his heart rate. He was looking for the zone—that nerveless place where the senses heightened and everything moved in slow motion.

He moved slowly toward Beverly's Hill, which was about fifty yards down the walkway. The Mossberg moved with his eyes as they swept the scene in front of him, looking for something out of place. Still no people; when Stephanie and he had been here before, there had been people. He passed a dilapidated house and saw two black faces behind an open window, staring at him. The people were here, but they were hiding.

Grant's eyes and the Mossberg continued to sweep from left to right. The bank rose up on his right, and buildings ran along his left. It would be easy to pick him off from anywhere. He slowly approached the steps to Beverly's Hill, stopped at the bottom, and looked up.

There were two brown middle-aged men at the top of the steps about fifty feet above him. Neither was holding a weapon, but Grant had no doubt their loose-fitting shirts covered their guns. From a combat point of view, they had the high ground, but with the Mossberg, he had superior firepower if he could get a little closer. He moved his head slightly and looked left and right. He saw nothing, but there had to be more than two of them. Someone could be behind him, and if so, he was dead.

The silence was shattered by his cell phone, which was in his chest pocket. Who in the hell would be calling? The men above were watching. What would they do if he answered the phone? Grant held the Mossberg in his right hand and reached for the phone with his left. It stopped ringing.

One of the men at the top of the steps called to Grant in heavily accented English. "Come up. Your woman is here."

No telling how many men were out of sight at the top of the hill, but Grant moved up a few steps and stopped. They were within the killing zone now.

"Bring her to the top of the stairs where I can see her."

The men looked at each other. "Let us see the money."

"It's in this duffel."

"Show us."

In order to do that, Grant would have to put down his shotgun. If they opened fire, he would be defenseless.

"Show me the woman first or I walk away from here."

"She is here, but we must see the money. Bring it to us."

Grant didn't like the way this was going. There was no reason not to bring Stephanie where he could see her. She may not even be there. It smelled like the trap he had worried about.

"You have ten seconds to show her to me or I leave."

The men looked at each other, and the one on the left jerked a pistol from the small of his back. Grant raised the Mossberg slightly and squeezed the trigger. The man with the gun flew backward and out of sight. The other man dropped and fired wildly at Grant. The Mossberg roared again and hit the top of the bank. Grant turned and ran for the dock. Stephanie wasn't here.

A man with a shotgun stepped from between some buildings twenty feet in front of him. Grant fired without breaking stride, blowing the man backward off his feet. He landed in the middle of the narrow walkway, and Grant leaped over him as gunfire erupted behind him, hitting the sidewalk and the buildings on his right.

Grant turned the corner and raced toward the dock and his boat, where two more men were waiting for him with drawn pistols. As their presence dawned on Grant and he began to slow, there was the unmistakable crack of a large-caliber weapon.

One of the men in front of him was struck from behind and blown into the water. The other man turned to see where the shot had come from as another round hit a piling next to him. Grant stopped, dropped the Mossberg, and pulled his Glock, adopting a two-handed shooter's stance. He fired, and the man dropped.

Grant resumed running toward his boat, with the duffel bag over his shoulder. Suddenly, the bag slammed into him, causing him to stagger sideways. A round had hit the duffel, and the money had stopped it from reaching Grant. As he regained his footing, the man he had shot started to rise from the pier. Grant ran to the man and shot him in the head.

Unexpectedly, Grant was knocked off his feet, as if someone with a baseball bat had hit his right leg from behind. His Glock went flying across the dock and into the water. More shots chipped the concrete around him, and the big gun boomed rapidly from somewhere offshore.

Grant reached for his leg and felt the stickiness. He looked at his hand; it was covered with bright-red blood. Hopefully the bullet had missed the femoral artery. One way or the other, he couldn't lie there with only the duffel for protection.

Trying to ignore what felt like a branding iron shoved deep into his leg, Grant slid off the pier and into the panga. He used the pier as a shield to untie his boat and start the motor. Several shots hit the dock and water around him. The big rifle boomed again and again.

Grant lay in the bottom of the panga as he swung it around. He pointed it out to sea and lay flat as he opened the throttle all the way. Quickly, the small-caliber shots stopped, and then the big gun went silent. He must be out of range.

A quarter mile later, he saw a panga with Turnbull and Delilah inside. Delilah was kneeling behind a huge rifle with a massive scope positioned on a tripod on the forward deck. She ignored Grant until Turnbull tapped her on the shoulder, and then she put down the rifle.

When Grant pulled alongside, she said, "Sorry 'bout the second guy; the boat rocked at the wrong time. Glad you took care uh him."

Grant nodded weakly. "Good work."

Turnbull looked closely at Grant. "What's wrong?"

Grant tried to pull himself onto the panga's seat but slipped back. He smiled weakly. "Got hit in the leg."

Turnbull started to move into Grant's panga, but Delilah pushed him aside. "Stay put, big boy. Let me see how bad it is."

Delilah swiftly moved into Grant's panga, despite her size. When Grant tried to sit up, she pushed him down while pulling the knife from his belt. She deftly cut away his pant leg and used the scrap to wipe off the blood around the wound.

"This here's the exit wound on the front part uh yer leg. It's a through and through. Missed the artery, thank the Lord. Don't look too bad, jus' went through muscle. You'll be okay."

Delilah used Grant's T-shirt to pad the front and back of the wound and bound it in place with strips of his other pant leg.

"Turnbull, you git on back to town and round up the EMT to meet us at the public dock. I'll bring this here cowboy along."

CHAPTER 43

The Bocas Town EMT cleaned, stitched, and bandaged Grant's wound on the town dock, shot him full of antibiotics, and gave him a bottle of Vicodin. Turnbull found a wheelchair somewhere, and they moved to a waterside table on the deck of the Bocas Hotel. Grant refused to take the Vicodin, not wanting to dull his senses yet.

"Yur bein' a fool again, Meredith," said Delilah between sips of beer. "Yuh let that pain get ahead a yuh and you'll pay hell gettin' it under control."

Grant ignored her.

The consensus was that the Mexicans would take care of their own dead and wounded, so there would be no police involvement. There was nothing to do but speculate about Stephanie's fate.

All of a sudden, they saw Scammon rushing across the deck, banging into chairs and tables in his haste. He arrived breathless.

"Grant, everybody, Stephanie is safe. Astrid called. Stephanie showed up in Bocas del Drago in a boat she had stolen from the kidnappers. Astrid's bringing her here right now."

Everyone started to talk at once. When would she be there? Had she been hurt? How had she escaped?

Finally, Scammon held up his hands. "Quiet! I don't know any more. They should be here shortly. I told Astrid to bring her here."

In the momentary quiet, Grant remembered the phone call that had come in while he was in Bastimentos. He pulled out his phone and played the message on the speaker.

"Grant, it's me, Stephanie. I escaped and ended up in Bocas del Drago. A woman named Astrid found me. She says she is a friend of someone named John Scammon and knew I was missing. Anyway, she let me use her phone and is giving me a ride to Bocas Town. I'll meet you at the Bocas Hotel. See you then."

Grant closed his eyes and slowly put the phone away. Then he smiled.

Grant's relief was indescribable but short-lived. Where was Stephanie? She should be here by now.

CHAPTER 44

There was only one narrow road from Bocas del Drago to Bocas Town, a distance of about fourteen miles. It was a pretty good road—narrow asphalt with sand blown across it in spots. Astrid was driving her faded red 1960 Volkswagen Beetle convertible and peppering Stephanie with nonstop questions.

Stephanie had cured her thirst at Astrid's, but in the convertible, the sun continued to bake her skin. The release from the tension of the last several days had left Stephanie feeling like a wet dishrag. What she wanted more than anything was to throw away the jeans and T-shirt she was wearing, drench her cracked lips in lip balm, take a long, hot shower, and get some sleep between crisp, clean sheets. She fought her weariness because until she was safely out of Bocas del Toro, her "vacation" was not over.

As she answered Astrid's questions in as few words as possible, her eyes moved from side to side across the roadway. From time to time she turned and looked behind them. The gangbangers were gone, but the man who called himself James Bond was a professional. Sooner or later he would find out what had happened to his men and come looking for her. That wasn't a pleasing prospect. She and Grant could get out of Panama, but what if Bond came looking for them? Neither of them would be hard to find; they would have to find Bond.

Astrid slowed to round a blind curve, and Stephanie saw in her side-view mirror an old Nissan pickup truck that had been sitting on the side of the road pull in behind them. Had the truck been waiting for them, or was it a coincidence? She looked forward again. A quarter mile later, a taxi pulled onto the road and stopped, facing the Volkswagen and blocking their lane of travel. Simultaneously, the pickup pulled alongside Astrid, blocking her in. Astrid hit the brakes, but the pickup slowed with her. The taxi sped directly toward them, and Astrid slammed on the brakes, sliding to a stop. The pickup driver deftly backed behind her left bumper, and the taxi blocked her from the front. They were trapped.

Astrid looked helplessly at Stephanie. Stephanie cursed herself for letting Astrid drive.

"Get out and run," yelled Stephanie as she pulled open her door, unwound her legs, and shoved them out the door, pulling herself to her feet.

The man who called himself James Bond had exited the taxi and was moving toward Stephanie. She could hear Astrid screaming in a language she didn't understand; then she heard the solid sound of something hitting flesh, followed by silence.

Bond, cocky as ever, sauntered toward Stephanie. When he was about twenty feet away, he said, "Not going to run, Ms. Chambers? I don't think you'll find me as easy as those two gangbangers."

His hands were empty—no gun. Although Stephanie was confident she could outrun him even though she was barefoot, she wanted to bring this nightmare to an end. She also had to think about Astrid.

She walked toward Bond and saw the surprise in his eyes. He didn't know what to expect, and that suited Stephanie just fine. As she approached, she moved as if to launch a kick toward his groin. Bond actually smiled as he moved his leg to protect himself and dropped a hand to grab Stephanie's foot. His throat was now exposed, and she drove her folded knuckles into his larynx with all the force she could muster. She felt his throat collapse.

Bond grabbed his throat with both hands and staggered in a small circle. Stephanie timed a perfect upthrust palm into his nose, and Bond dropped like a stone.

Stephanie turned Bond over, and, as she had suspected, there was a Glock 16 in the waistband of his pants. She grabbed the gun and whirled around, searching for Astrid. A short, fat black man with dreadlocks was dropping her into the bed of the small pickup. Stephanie walked slowly toward him.

Without turning, the man said, "Got this one. Did you finish the bitch?"

Stephanie kept walking toward him. The man turned and looked incredulously at Stephanie, and then he looked around frantically for Bond. He moved to meet Stephanie, and she raised the Glock and shot him in the forehead. The sound of a gunshot was so out of place in Bocas that Stephanie hoped anyone who heard it wouldn't know what it was.

In three minutes Stephanie had moved the taxi and truck to the side of the road and stuffed Bond and the dreadlocked man in the taxi's trunk. Astrid, holding her head and groaning, was slumped in the passenger seat of the Volkswagen as Stephanie drove toward town, carefully staying within the speed limit and thanking her lucky stars that no one had come along while she cleaned up the bodies.

As she drove to town, the fact that she had killed four people in this foreign country settled in her mind. There was absolutely no regret or second-guessing what she had done. There had been no choice, but that didn't mean the police and the locals would see it that way. Three of the dead had probably lived in Bocas, and Bond had worked for a drug cartel, which was undoubtedly connected. More importantly, the cartel was still there and would try to exact revenge. Grant had better have a plane with the engine running.

CHAPTER 45

Astrid leaned heavily on Stephanie as she led her through the lobby and onto the Bocas Hotel's waterside deck. Bedlam broke out when Stephanie saw Grant in a wheelchair. She rushed to him, while Scammon hurried to Astrid.

"Grant, my God, what happened?"

"I'll tell you later. We've got to get out of here. What happened to Astrid?"

Stephanie quickly explained about running into Bond on the road. "I'll fill you in on the rest later. I want out of this place."

Grant called the pilot amid the confusion and gestured for everyone to be quiet. "How long ago were they there? What did they look like? What did he say? Okay, we'll be there in a few minutes. Get yourself ready to take off immediately."

"What's up?" asked Turnbull.

"The pilot says a couple cops were at the airport this morning, checking his papers and asking who he was waiting for. As he described them, one was probably Noriega. Look, let's get going. I want out of here before Noriega comes back to the airport. For all I know, he may be mixed up in this."

"Hold on, Grant," said Delilah. "Noriega knows who yuh are. If any uh Stephanie's handiwork has turned up, you'll be at the top uh his list. The first place he'll look is the airport."

"I can borrow a pretty fast ocean fishing boat. You two could stay below deck until we get out of the harbor. Costa Rica's only a couple hours away," said Turnbull.

Grant groaned involuntarily.

"Grant, for God's sake, I tole yuh to take one of dem pills. Yuh is jes makin' yurself miserable," said Delilah.

Grant swallowed another burst of pain. A tear leaked from the corner of his eye, and he brushed it away. "Stephanie, we've got to get out of here. You killed four men. There are four more bodies at Old Town and two in the ocean. If that idiot Noriega arrests us, we may never get out of here. What do you think about the boat?"

"I don't know, Grant. I want to get out of here as fast as I can. All the plane has to do is get in the air. We can be in the air in ten minutes, maybe less" said Stephanie.

Astrid started shaking and would have collapsed if Scammon hadn't grabbed her and eased her into a chair.

"Astrid, what's the matter?" asked Scammon, kneeling beside her.

"Oh, Lord," said Astrid with her head in her hands. "Don't get on no airplane, please don't. I had an awful vision: an airplane and then nothing but white light. Don't get on no airplane."

Scammon looked at Grant and then Stephanie. "She has a gift. Sometimes she can see around corners...but I don't know. The harbor patrol has a really fast boat. I just don't know. With the plane, like Stephanie says, you can be airborne in just a few minutes."

CHAPTER 46

Twenty minutes later, the plane Grant had chartered lifted off from the Bocas Town Airport and made a graceful arc north toward Costa Rica. Noriega stood on the town dock, smoking a cigarette and watching as the plane gained altitude.

Suddenly, an explosion shattered the air, and the plane burst into flames. A few seconds later, whatever was left of the plane disappeared from view.

Noriega took a last drag on his cigarette and crushed it underfoot, a sly smile on his face. Another payday like this one and he could retire.

CHAPTER 47

A massive explosion shattered the quiet of Bocas del Toro, and the plane disappeared in a ball of fire. Turnbull looked up from the wheel of a powerful boat racing out of the Bocas harbor and shook his head.

Grant was in the berth below, heading toward la-la land on Vicodin. He didn't move.

Stephanie came up from below. "What happened?"

Turnbull just shook his head in disbelief.

"Astrid's prophecy came true. Girl, I reckon you cud use a drink 'bout now," Delilah said.

CHAPTER 48

The next day, Grant and Stephanie lifted off from Costa Rica in a BlackRock plane for the flight home.

"You know, Grant, we're going to have to worry about Guzman. He's likely to look for revenge; it's something the cartels specialize in."

Grant sipped a seventeen-year-old single malt, rubbed his wound, and said, "Maybe. Let's think about that later. There's one thing I forgot to tell you. When I was desperate, I learned that Hector Sanchez was in Panama City for a conference. I went to see him for help. He didn't offer any, but he called a day later. I didn't take the call, but I'm thinking he must have had some news or something to say."

Stephanie shrugged. "Does it matter now?"

She picked up the *New York Times* off the table and settled back. She flipped the paper to the bottom of the first page and stared at the headline: "El Chapo, Most Wanted Drug Lord, Captured in Mexico."

Stephanie handed the paper to Grant. "This is why Hector called."

Grant shook his head slowly. "Maybe there is justice after all. But then again, it's Mexico."